Darcie looked up pa̶ . . . . had ever seen and int . . . . eyes of the new boarder.

Oh. He's very handsome, his dark hair parted slightly to the left of center, his clean-shaven face nicely chiseled. . . .

Darcie's heart beat faster when she realized he might be here awhile, then promptly slowed as she reminded herself awhile was not forever. He had business here, and then he'd be gone. But what if—

"Harper, you say?" Mr. Mitchell asked.

"Yes, sir."

"Not any kin to Douglas Harper, are you?"

Harper, Harper. Why hadn't she made the connection? Darcie wondered, as she held her breath, waiting for the man's answer.

"Why, yes, I am. He was my uncle, and I came out here to settle his estate."

The dream Darcie was weaving crumbled as suddenly as her heart plunged to her feet. She felt as if the breath had been knocked plumb out of her. She should have known.

White-hot anger she hadn't been aware she still harbored welled up from deep within her. She looked down the length of the table. "Mama! How could you rent a room to any relative of Douglas Harper?"

"Darcie Malone. You'll not talk to me like that." Color flooded her mother's face.

Darcie couldn't keep the words from escaping her lips. "But how could you?"

JANET LEE BARTON has lived all over the southern U.S., but she and her husband plan to stay put in southern Mississippi, where they have made their home for the past ten years. With three daughters and six grandchildren between them, they feel blessed to have at least one daughter and her family living in the same town. Janet loves being able to share her faith through her writing. Happily married to her very own hero, she is ever thankful that the Lord brought Dan into her life, and she wants to write stories that show that the love between a man and a woman is at its best when the relationship is built with God at the center. She's very happy that the kind of romances the Lord has called her to write can be read by and shared with women of all ages, from teenagers to grand-mothers alike.

Books by Janet Lee Barton

HEARTSONG PRESENTS
HP434—Family Circle
HP532—A Promise Made
HP562—Family Ties
HP623—A Place Called Home

Making Amends

Janet Lee Barton

Heartsong Presents

To my Lord and Savior for showing me the way, the family I was born into, and the family the Lord has given me. I love you all.

A note from the Author:
I love to hear from my readers! You may correspond with me by writing:

Janet Lee Barton
Author Relations
PO Box 719
Uhrichsville, OH 44683

ISBN 1-59310-527-4

MAKING AMENDS

All scripture quotations are taken from the King James Version of the Bible.

PRINTED IN THE U.S.A.

one

Late March 1899—Roswell, New Mexico Territory

The train pulled to a stop in Roswell, New Mexico Territory, and Attorney John Harper stood and stretched. It had been a long trip from Georgia, and he was glad it had come to an end. He dusted off the shoulders of his jacket, gathered his bags, and got in line to leave the passenger car. Stepping off the train, he was struck by how wide the cloudless blue sky seemed out here and how much closer than back home.

John started toward the train depot, more than a little surprised at the size of Roswell. From what his father had told him about the town, he hadn't expected it to be as large or as busy as it was. He'd thought he could get off the train and immediately find the office of the lawyer who had written to let him know he was his uncle's only heir. Instead he found a bustling town filled with people going about the day's business.

John did not even know his uncle, Douglas Harper. Moreover, from his father's account of his uncle, John could not understand why the man had left anything at all to him. The two brothers had not been on good terms for years. John had heard enough to know his uncle Douglas had been smitten with his mother, but she had not felt the same about him. According to John's grandmother, there was never a question of which brother would win the heart of her daughter, Margaret. Grandmother Smithfield had told John many times that his mother had fallen in love with James Harper

5

the first moment she saw him.

Evidently Uncle Douglas had not taken her decision well. He'd left Georgia and traveled west to make his fortune, never to return. He refused to come back even when James had gone out to plead with him to return for the sake of their dying father.

John sighed deeply and shook his head. He did not know how his uncle had died, nor did he understand why Douglas Harper had named him in his will. He only knew he needed to find the lawyer who had written him, visit his uncle's gravesite, and learn what had happened to him.

John crossed the boardwalk that led to the train depot, opened the door, and strolled up to the counter.

"May I help you?" the man behind the counter asked.

John smiled. "I hope you can. My name is John Harper, and I'm looking for my uncle's lawyer, a Mr. Elmer Griffin."

"You Douglas Harper's nephew?" The man behind the counter's right eyebrow crept up into his hairline.

"Yes, sir, I am. Did you know my uncle?" John could not help but notice an abrupt change in the man's demeanor.

"Not well. Elmer's office is over on Fifth Street, across from the courthouse." With that, the clerk leaned to the side and looked at the woman next in line. "May I help you, ma'am?"

"Would it be all right if I leave my valises here until I have a place to stay?" John asked, feeling as if he suddenly didn't exist.

"Here—give them to me," the clerk said gruffly and went to the end of the counter.

John handed his bags to the man. "Thank you."

The man grunted. John knew when he had been snubbed. He walked out of the office and blinked his eyes against the bright sunlight before realizing he hadn't asked which way Fifth Street was. But he certainly didn't want to go back in the depot and ask the clerk. An old-timer was sitting in a chair leaning up against the building. John approached him with a smile; he'd always had a soft spot for old people.

"How do, sir. I'm John Harper, and I'm looking for the office of Elmer Griffin. I was told it's on Fifth Street, but I'm new to the area and don't know where that is."

"Old Elmer don't do much business these days. 'Bout the only business he's handled lately is Douglas Harper's."

"Yes! That's who I'm looking for. Douglas Harper was my uncle."

"You don't say?"

"Yes. Did you know him?"

"I knew 'im." The older man sat up straight, plunking the chair down on its four legs, and pointed to the right. "Fifth Street is over that way a couple of blocks. Elmer has a sign out front—you won't miss it."

"Thank you." John tipped the brim of his hat to the man, but again he felt dismissed. The old man had already leaned back against the building and closed his eyes.

John started down the street in the direction the man had told him to go. The main street was full of surreys, farm wagons, and freight wagons, and people rushed in all directions. So far no one he'd met had been friendly. Neither of the two men had given him condolences about his uncle passing away; in fact, his very name seemed to put up a barrier of some kind.

He wondered why people would change as soon as they heard he was a relation of Douglas Harper. That seemed odd to John because, in his few letters home, his uncle had painted himself as one of the most important and influential men in Roswell.

The law office of Elmer Griffin was across from the courthouse, as he'd been told. It was a small office with a big sign outside. He opened the door and stepped inside to see a rotund man leaning back in a chair behind a massive desk, his feet propped up on it, his head resting on his chest. He emitted a snore so loud that John jumped back a step.

It was midmorning, and the man was asleep. Business must be slow. John cleared his throat from inside the door. The snoring only grew louder. He moved to the center of the room and cleared his throat again.

The rumbling snort stopped briefly, then started again. John walked closer to the desk and cleared his throat as loudly as he could. The large man stirred. John leaned toward him. "Excuse me, sir?"

This time he started. His eyes opened, and he jerked his feet off the desk. "Humph! Yes? Who are you? What can I do for you?"

"I'm John Harper." He pulled out a letter. "I believe you sent me this letter."

The man was on his feet in an instant. He reached across the desk and extended his hand. "Mr. Harper. Yes, I'm Elmer Griffin. I trust you had a good trip out?"

John shook his hand. "It was fine, all things considered. A little hot and dusty. Still, train travel is better than stagecoach or horseback."

"Yes, yes, I agree." Elmer Griffin motioned to the chair on the other side of the desk. "Please take a seat, Mr. Harper. As you know from my letter, your uncle named you as his only heir. His money has been placed in trust, and I am the trustee. Now that money belongs to you." He pushed his glasses up on his nose. "It is a sizable sum."

John's breath caught in his throat when Mr. Griffin named the amount.

"He was an astute businessman," he added as if in explanation.

"I'd say he was." His uncle had been a rich man.

"We can go to the Roswell Bank and transfer the funds to you as soon as you are ready. Other than that, I'm sure you have questions you would like answered."

"Well, yes, I do. First and foremost I'd like to know how my uncle died." John sat down in the chair and watched Elmer Griffin wipe his brow with a handkerchief he'd pulled from his coat pocket. The man seemed nervous to him.

"Well, he. . .ah. . .he died from the influenza. It swept through the prison, and before they could get a doctor in, five prisoners had died."

"My uncle was in prison? Why—and for how long?" This was news to him and would be to his family. He sat forward on the edge of the chair.

Elmer Griffin cleared his throat. "Yes, well, he died a couple of months ago. He was in the jail here—until his trial for arson. He was found guilty of hiring someone to set fire to Emma's Café. He was sentenced to five years in prison, but he had only served about a year and a half of that time when he fell ill."

John sat silent, trying to take in what his uncle's attorney was telling him. No wonder he had not been welcomed in the town with open arms. Apparently his uncle was not the fine upstanding man he had led the family to believe he was. On the rare occasion he had been in contact with them, he had indicated he was one of Roswell's leading citizens. And even though his father and his uncle hadn't been close, John wondered why his uncle Douglas hadn't contacted the family law firm when he got into trouble.

He looked at the older man. "You defended him?"

Elmer Griffin nodded. "Yes, I defended him—but only because the court ordered me to do so."

"Do you think he was guilty?"

The older man shrugged. "I don't know. Someone came forward and admitted he lit the fire—and said Harper hired him to do it. Your uncle did not have many people on his side, Mr. Harper. He treated some of the people in Roswell and in the surrounding area badly."

Suddenly John wasn't sure he wanted to find out how badly, and he had an urge to take the first train back to Georgia. But he knew he wouldn't do that. He wasn't that kind of man. He'd stay and get to the bottom of this—he had no choice, now that he'd been named his uncle's heir.

"I hope you are a better man than your uncle was, sir." The man let out a deep sigh. John had a feeling the lawyer had been dreading this meeting for a long time.

"I did not know my uncle, Mr. Griffin. But from what you've told me, it appears my family name is at stake here. I will do what I can to restore honor to it. I'm not sure, though, where to start."

Elmer Griffin looked at him closely before nodding. "If you mean that, I'll do what I can to help you, Mr. Harper."

"Please call me John."

"All right, John. And call me Elmer. You're taking on a large task. I hope you'll be able to stay and see it through."

"I'm a member of the family law firm. My father has told me to take as long as I need to settle my uncle's estate."

The older man looked in his desk drawer and pulled out a key. He stood up and handed it to John. "Your uncle's office at Harper Bank would probably be the best place to start. It has been closed down ever since he went to prison."

"What about the people who did business there? Were they able to get their money out?"

Elmer nodded. "The sheriff saw to it that they were able

to do that before Harper went to trial. But I feel I must warn you—those who still owe money to your uncle probably won't be glad to see you. Just be sure you look over those papers with a fine-tooth comb. All may not be what it seems at first glance."

John took the key and slipped it into his pocket. "Can you tell me where the bank is?"

"I'll do better than that. I'll go with you. It'll be time to eat in a few hours. I'll treat you to a meal at the Roswell Hotel. It's not far from the bank."

"Thank you." Not looking forward to the task at hand, John was glad to have the company of the older man. "I appreciate your help."

*

Elmer showed John where his uncle's office was inside the bank and left with the promise of returning at noontime. After seeing him out, John walked back to the file cabinet behind his uncle's desk and pulled out several file folders. Plunking them down on the desk, he sat down and opened the top one.

After only a couple of hours, John realized how right Elmer was. A huge job was unfolding before him. It would take weeks to go over his uncle's papers.

True to his word, Elmer returned and treated him to dinner. John was impressed with the quality of food and service at the Roswell Hotel. But he wasn't sure he wanted to stay there. Leaning back in his chair, he smiled at Elmer. "Thank you. That was a wonderful meal."

"You're quite welcome. Are you going back to the office now? Have you decided on a place to stay? I've heard the accommodations here are very nice. It's where your uncle lived. Had the nicest suite in the place."

John briefly wondered why his uncle had chosen to live in a hotel instead of a home of his own, but he supposed it was fairly common for single men to do that, especially when they had no family around. He shook his head to Elmer's first question. "No, I'll go back to the office first thing in the morning. I guess the most important item of business for me now is to find a place to stay. I had thought to stay in a hotel, but it looks as though I'll be here awhile. Nice as this place seems to be, I think I might be more comfortable in a boardinghouse. Can you recommend any?"

"We have several in town, and they list their vacancies in the paper. Let me go find you a copy." He came back shortly with the morning paper in hand, turned to the inside, then handed John the advertisements.

John skimmed the page. "There's a room at the Roswell Inn, one at Malone's Boardinghouse, and another one at Brady's Boardinghouse."

"Oh, Molly Malone's is a great place to stay. She's a wonderful cook, and I've heard only good things about her establishment," Elmer said. "I'd try there first."

"I'll see if a room is still available. Can you tell me how to get there?"

After giving him directions to the boardinghouse, Elmer took his leave, assuring John once more that he would be glad to help in any way he could. They made plans to meet the next morning at the Harper Bank.

❧

Darcie Malone shook hands with her supervisor, Mr. McQuillen, thrilled she'd just been given a promotion. She left his office with a grin on her face but let out a sigh as soon as she returned to her station. She had gone into his office thinking he was about to reprimand her for listening in on conversations again. Instead she'd come out as the head operator, in charge of training for the Roswell Telephone and Manufacturing Company. She suppressed the excited giggle that wanted release and took her seat at the switchboard.

She wasn't sure she believed it yet! Oh, she knew that with her best friend, Beth, now married and no longer working, she might be next in line for a promotion. But she'd been reprimanded so many times, she'd feared that would keep her from getting it. The few extra dollars she would make a month would certainly help her mother. They wouldn't be enough, though, for her to turn their house back into a private home instead of a boardinghouse. Darcie sighed. Maybe one day.

She plugged the line pin into her home socket and pulled the lever. She didn't want to wait until she got home to tell her good news. Her mother worked so hard; hearing a little more money would be coming in might make her tasks easier today.

Her mother picked up the receiver on the third ring. "Malone's Boardinghouse. How may I help you?"

"It's me, Mama. I have some good news to share with you."

"Oh? What is it, dear?"

Darcie could picture her mother's bright smile. "Well, as of tomorrow, I will be the head operator at Roswell Telephone and Manufacturing Company. It means a little more money coming in."

"Oh, you're right—that is very good news, Darcie! I'm so proud of you, dear."

"Thank you." Tears came to Darcie's eyes at her mother's words. She never held back on her praise for her daughter.

"I have some news of my own. We have a new boarder as of this afternoon."

"Wonderful!" Darcie could hear the excitement in her mother's voice, and she had to force herself to sound happy. It meant one more stranger to get used to in her home, not to mention more work for her mother. But the older woman wouldn't welcome her daughter's attitude, so Darcie tried to hide it the best she could.

"He seems like a nice young man. You'll meet him at dinner. I put a roast on earlier. I'm glad it's your favorite meal, since we must celebrate your promotion and a new boarder all in one day!"

Several lights on her switchboard lit up. "I must get back to work, Mama. I'll see you in a few hours." She pulled the pin from her home line, knowing her mother would understand the quick end to their conversation, and inserted a pin into the plug of one of the lighted lines. "Number, please."

"I need to talk to Emma, over at the café, Darcie."

Darcie recognized the voice of Matt Johnson, Emma's husband and a deputy sheriff. "Right away, Deputy."

She inserted his line pin into the line for Emma's Café and waited for an answer before turning her attention to the next lighted line. As she went about connecting and disconnecting telephone lines, her thoughts turned back to her promotion. She had only a few more hours to go on her shift—and tomorrow she would have a completely new job. More and more people were signing up for telephone service, and Mr. McQuillen had hired two new operators who were due to start the next day. It would be Darcie's job to train them. She sent up a silent prayer that she would do a good job and be a good example to them, as Beth had been to her.

ಶ

Heading back to the train depot to pick up his bags, John left Malone's Boardinghouse with a spring in his step. Mrs.

Malone's establishment was warm and inviting, and the smell coming from her kitchen reminded him of his mother's at home. The room she'd rented him was large and bright, overlooking the large cottonwood in the front yard. She was also the friendliest person he'd met in this town so far. He wasn't looking forward to his task of settling his uncle's estate, but for whatever time he was here, he would be comfortable.

two

As soon as her shift was over and the evening operator showed up to relieve her, Darcie left for home. She hoped the friends she'd made at the telephone office would be happy about her promotion when they found out. She did not want to appear to be boasting about it and decided she would let Mr. McQuillen announce it the next morning as he planned.

As Darcie entered her home, she couldn't help but feel pride that it had become the best boardinghouse in town, even though she would have preferred it to remain a private home. Everyone who stayed there had commented on how warm and homey it was.

Of course she agreed. Her mother had decorated tastefully, from the downstairs to each room upstairs, and there wasn't a room Darcie didn't like.

The front parlor was done in gold and blue flowered wall coverings. It was furnished with a parlor set covered in gold silk damask, and burgundy silk draperies hung at the doorway and windows. The room was a favorite of the boarders. A chess set stood waiting for Mr. Mitchell and Mr. Carlton to continue their game later in the evening. The back parlor was finished in mostly deep rose with touches of gold and seemed to draw the women to sit and do needlework or read during the evenings.

Miss Olivia Waterford and Mr. Mitchell were in the front parlor, reading the newspaper, and Darcie waved at them before hurrying to the kitchen to see if her mother needed help putting dinner on the table. She marveled at how her mother managed to look fresh and energetic after spending a good portion of the day over a hot stove. In her mid-forties, she still had a trim figure and always dressed neatly, a crisp apron protecting her clothing. Although her red hair was beginning to fade a little, her blue eyes seemed brighter with age.

Her mother was taking the roast out of the oven when Darcie entered the kitchen. She looked up with a smile. "There you are. The new head operator—I am so proud of you, dear."

"Thank you, Mama. It smells wonderful in here. You must have been cooking all afternoon."

Her mother set the roast on the kitchen table and pointed to the cake beside it. "We have good reason to celebrate tonight, what with your promotion and all! I made that chocolate cake you like so much for dessert tonight, too."

Darcie walked over and gave her mother a hug. "Thank you. But you shouldn't have worked so hard."

"It's not work when it's for someone you love, dear. Did you see the new boarder when you came in?"

"No. Only Miss Olivia and Mr. Mitchell were talking in the parlor."

"He is probably settling in. He had to go back to the train station to pick up his valises after he rented the room. He seems to be a nice gentleman."

"That's good. I just wish we—"

"Darcie, dear, I do understand how you feel. Still, we need to be thankful we had this house to turn into a business and can earn a living from it. Besides, I really do enjoy it. I know that's hard for you to believe, but it would be very lonesome with only myself for company when you're at work."

It was hard for her to believe, but out of respect for her

mother, she smiled and hugged her again. "I know you're right, Mama. I need to be more thankful for my blessings. I do thank the Lord for them—I really do." And she did—maybe not as often as she should, though. Darcie promised herself she would do better. "Now—what do you need me to do?"

"You can put vegetables on the table and the cake and dessert plates on the sideboard."

Darcie dished up the roasted potatoes, carrots, and onions into serving bowls and took them to the dining table. She loved this room. Scarlet upholstered chairs and scarlet draperies with gold trim enhanced the gold and scarlet printed wallpaper. The table was covered with an ivory lace tablecloth and set with her mother's best china. Darcie thought it was the most elegant room in the house.

She could hear more voices in the parlor as she put dessert plates on the sideboard and briefly wondered if the new boarder had come downstairs. Her mother carried out the meat dish and a gravy boat as Darcie went back for the cake. Just as she reentered the dining room, she could hear her mother calling the boarders to the table.

Darcie stood at her place at the opposite end of the table from where her mother would sit and smiled as the guests entered the room to take their seats.

"Darcie, dear, I'd like you to meet John Harper, our newest boarder. He's a lawyer and will be here for at least a month or so. Mr. Harper, this is my daughter, Darcie Marie."

Darcie looked up past the broadest shoulders she had ever seen and into the deep chocolate-colored eyes of the new boarder. *Oh. He's very handsome, his dark hair parted slightly to the left of center, his clean-shaven face nicely chiseled. . . .* Just looking at him left her breathless.

"How do you do, Miss Malone?"

Darcie could feel her cheeks growing warm as she stood there. She forced the air out of her lungs. "I—I'm fine, thank you. And you?"

"Very well, thank you." He smiled at her, then inclined his head in her mother's direction. "And I've become quite hungry smelling this food your mother has prepared for us."

Everyone else had taken his or her seat at the table. Three chairs had been empty at the table for eight, and her mother had hoped for new boarders to fill them. The one to Darcie's left had remained vacant since Mrs. Green had moved out. Darcie was pleased when she realized the new boarder would be sitting next to her. He pulled out her chair and waited for her to sit. She only hoped he could not hear the rapid beating of her heart—for it was quite loud to her own ears.

Darcie tried to will her heartbeat to slow its pace as she sat down. She was relieved when her mother spoke.

"Before I ask Mr. Mitchell to say the blessing, I have an announcement to make. Darcie has been promoted to head operator at the Roswell Telephone and Manufacturing Company."

"What wonderful news, Darcie!" Miss Olivia said. She'd lived at the boardinghouse for over a year. She had come out west to take care of her ailing sister and moved in after she passed away.

"They made a good decision in promoting you, Miss Darcie," Robert Mitchell added. He'd been living at the boardinghouse for about six months and was overseeing the railroad expansion.

"They certainly did." George Carlton nodded from his place to the right of her mother. Mr. Carlton taught school and had resided with them ever since he'd come to Roswell two years earlier.

"May I add my congratulations?" Mr. Harper asked.

"Thank you." Darcie had to force herself to look away from his warm gaze. "Thank you all. I'm a little nervous about it, but I'm very pleased, too."

"You'll do fine," her mother said, beaming at her. "Just fine. Now let's not let this meal get cold. Mr. Mitchell, please ask a blessing for us."

Darcie bowed her head and tried to keep her mind on his words.

"Dear Lord, thank You for this day and for Darcie's promotion. And thank You for the food we are about to eat. In Jesus' name, amen."

Her mother always complained about Mr. Mitchell's prayers being much too short, but he pouted if she didn't take turns asking him and Mr. Carlton. Hard as it was for Darcie to think about anything except the man at her left, she thought maybe it was just right tonight.

As the dishes were passed around the table, she tried to concentrate on the conversation.

"Ahh, beef with roasted potatoes and carrots. I think this is one of my favorite meals, Mrs. Malone," Mr. Carlton said.

"Thank you," her mother said.

Darcie glanced down at the table as she saw the wink her mother flashed her. She tried to hide her smile behind her napkin. Every meal her mother cooked was one of Mr. Carlton's favorites.

She looked up and found Mr. Harper watching her, a smile hovering around his lips as if he understood the unspoken conversation between the two women.

"Oh, dear," her mother said, her hand at her chest. "With the excitement of Darcie's promotion, I'm afraid I've forgotten my manners. Have you all met our new boarder, John Harper?"

"I have," Mr. Mitchell said.

Miss Olivia patted her graying fluff of hair and nodded. "Yes, I did—this afternoon. I was sitting in the parlor reading when he arrived. It's always nice to meet new lodgers."

"Pleased to meet you," Mr. Carlton said with a nod. "You'll find no better food in all of Roswell."

Mr. Harper smiled and nodded. "I've been told that. But even if I hadn't heard, I would have known when I came by to inquire about the vacancy. When I stepped inside and smelled the aroma coming from the kitchen, it reminded me of my mother's kitchen. I knew I'd come to the right place."

"Why, Mr. Harper, thank you," her mother said. "I'll take that as a high compliment."

He nodded in her direction. "As it was meant to be."

Darcie could tell her mother was pleased, and her opinion of the new boarder inched upward at the way he treated her—with respect and honor. She'd been through so much. Having her husband die from a sudden stroke, then losing all he'd worked so hard for—with the exception of the house in town, which they'd been able to turn into a way of making ends meet. Having to give up her privacy and the kind of life she'd become accustomed to through the years couldn't have been easy. Darcie gave herself a mental shake. No. She couldn't start thinking about the past. It never failed to bring tears to her eyes, and then her mother would tear up.

*

Mrs. Malone began to pass the dishes around so the boarders could help themselves, and quiet reigned at the table for a few minutes while they began to eat. John told himself to be sure to thank Elmer Griffin for suggesting the Malone boardinghouse. The food was excellent, and so far everyone seemed amiable. He would be comfortable here for his stay.

Not to mention Mrs. Malone's daughter. He hadn't been prepared for the jolt of awareness he'd felt when he walked into the dining room and found her standing at the end of the table.

With her shining auburn hair and sparkling blue-green eyes, she was very lovely, and he'd found it hard to keep his eyes off her. To keep from gazing at her now, he tried to concentrate on the dinner conversation going on around him.

"I think being a telephone operator would be so interesting, Darcie. Don't you just love it?" Miss Waterford asked. She looked to be a little younger than Mrs. Malone. Perhaps in her late thirties, he thought.

"Yes, Miss Olivia, I do love working for the telephone company."

Miss Waterford nodded. "If I were younger, I'd apply for a position there. Isn't it amazing that one can talk to someone clear across town? That is so hard for me to believe."

"Oh, nowadays one can even talk to people outside town— even to Eddy and more," Darcie said with a smile for the older woman.

"You don't say?" Miss Waterford asked, holding her hand to her chest. She sighed. "So many new inventions to make life easier for us. What a wonderful time we live in."

John felt ashamed for thinking the pace of life wasn't moving fast enough. He'd wanted to place a call to his parents earlier and found that long distance in Roswell extended only a hundred miles or so.

"Why, some places make connections out farther than that. One of these days, I predict we'll be able to talk to people clear across the country," Mr. Mitchell said.

Miss Waterford gasped. "You don't say!"

"It's only a matter of time," Mr. Carlton agreed, handing

John a basket of rolls. "Isn't that right, Miss Darcie?"

"Oh, yes, I'm sure it is," Darcie answered. "Lines are being strung daily, and they go farther out each week. In fact, the Roswell Telephone and Manufacturing Company hired two more linemen a week or so ago."

She was so animated while she talked about the company. When she caught his gaze on her, John felt flustered at the warmth in her eyes, and his heart pounded in his chest. He held out the bread basket. "Would you like a roll, Miss Darcie?"

"Thank you, yes."

❧

Darcie took the basket from him, and their fingers brushed, sending a tingly sensation up her forearm.

"Pass the gravy, please, Darcie," Mr. Mitchell asked.

She picked up the gravy boat in front of her and handed it to the older man, silently sighing with relief that her hands didn't shake. Darcie had never felt so attracted to a man as she was to John Harper, and she was flustered by the way her pulse raced at his nearness. He was so handsome and seemed very nice. Just the kind of man she'd always dreamed of—

"How long did you say you'd be with us?" Mr. Carlton inquired of Mr. Harper, cutting into Darcie's thoughts. She listened closely to the answer.

"I'm not sure. Several weeks, a month or two—possibly longer. I don't know yet," he said.

Darcie's heart beat faster when she realized he might be here awhile, then promptly slowed as she reminded herself awhile was not forever. He had business here, and then he'd be gone. But what if—

"Harper, you say?" Mr. Mitchell asked.

"Yes, sir."

"Not any kin to Douglas Harper, are you?"

Harper, Harper. Why hadn't she made the connection? Darcie wondered, as she held her breath, waiting for the man's answer.

"Why, yes, I am. He was my uncle, and I came out here to settle his estate."

The dream Darcie was weaving crumbled as suddenly as her heart plunged to her feet. She felt as if the breath had been knocked plumb out of her. She should have known.

White-hot anger she hadn't been aware she still harbored welled up from deep within her. She looked down the length of the table. "Mama! How could you rent a room to any relative of Douglas Harper?"

"Darcie Malone. You'll not talk to me like that." Color flooded her mother's face.

Darcie couldn't keep the words from escaping her lips. "But how could you?"

Her mother pushed back her chair and stood. "I'll have a word with you in the kitchen. Now."

Darcie knew not to argue with that tone; she realized she'd gone too far. She pushed back her own chair and headed toward the kitchen.

Before leaving the room, her mother turned and spoke to those seated around the table. "Please excuse us and go on with your meal."

Darcie braced herself for the admonishment she knew she deserved and had no doubt was coming.

❧

John Harper wasn't sure what to do as Mrs. Malone and her daughter left the table. What had his uncle done to the Malone family to cause such an outburst? And should he stay or go?

Mr. Carlton and Miss Waterford were both looking at him suspiciously. If only he knew why the people in this town reacted so negatively at the mere mention of Douglas Harper's name. At the same time, he dreaded finding out.

The other boarders made small talk among themselves, and he tried to concentrate on that instead of the rise and fall of voices coming from the kitchen. Although he couldn't hear what was being said, John was certain he was the topic of conversation.

Mr. Mitchell cleared his throat and held out the platter of meat as if it were a peace offering. "Would you like more beef?"

John shook his head. He probably couldn't finish what was on his plate. "No, thank you."

He took a bite of roasted potatoes and found they didn't taste as good as they had only moments before. In fact, he had to struggle to swallow. He laid down his fork and took a drink of water. When he looked up, all eyes were focused on him. John put his napkin on the table and pushed away from the table.

"If you'll excuse me, I believe I'll call it a night."

"You aren't staying for some of Molly's chocolate cake?" Miss Waterford asked. "It's a favorite for all of us."

"No, ma'am. I'm a little tired from the travel. I won't wait for Mrs. Malone to come back, but please tell her I thought the meal was delicious."

"Yes, we will do that," Mr. Carlton said.

John turned and left the room, but before he was out of earshot, he could hear the whispers of the others. *Talking about me, no doubt.*

three

Darcie could tell by the way her mother marched across the kitchen and looked out the back door that she was trying to compose herself. She tried to swallow around the huge lump in her throat. She felt awful, realizing she'd caused her mother to be so upset. But she still couldn't believe Douglas Harper's nephew had rented a room in their home.

Her mother turned to face her, unshed tears in her eyes. She shook her head. "I cannot believe you humiliated us both in such a way, Darcie. I—"

Darcie looked down, trying to keep her own tears at bay. "Mama, I'm sorry I spoke the way I did and that I didn't wait until we were alone." She glanced up. "But I can't believe you rented a room to the nephew of the man who put us through so much misery!"

"Darcie, dear, you must realize I didn't know he was Douglas Harper's nephew when I rented the room to him. But—"

"Of course you didn't!" Darcie sighed with relief that her mother hadn't knowingly rented to the enemy. "Then you must tell him to find another place to stay. There are plenty of hotels in town. Let him stay at one of them! I'll be glad to tell him for you, Mama."

Her mother shook her head. "No, we'll not do that, Darcie. He is not to blame for the sins of his uncle. And we need the money."

"Only because of his uncle."

"Darcie, John Harper has done us no harm. And until it becomes apparent he intends to, I will keep my agreement with him. He will be staying with us for as long as he is in town—unless you've insulted him so badly, he decides to seek other accommodations. I expect you to apologize to him and the other boarders for your rudeness just now."

"But, Mama—" Darcie paused. "He is still the nephew of the man who put Papa under so much stress that he had a stroke! How can we allow him to stay here?"

"Darcie, Douglas Harper is dead. He can't hurt us anymore. And his nephew is not responsible for his uncle's actions. You didn't see the look on his face at your outburst. I'm sure he doesn't even know why you are so upset, and he deserves an apology."

Darcie knew he did. Still, it would be one of the hardest things she'd ever done. She had no idea how she would stand having a relation of the man she held responsible for her father's death living under her mother's roof.

"Darcie—" Her mother paused, waiting for Darcie's response.

"Yes, ma'am. I will apologize for being rude. And I do truly apologize to you, Mama. I am sorry I hurt you in any way."

Her mother drew her toward her in a hug. "I know you are. And I understand your pain. But, Darcie, dear—you must learn to forgive. It's what I pray for daily."

The tears in Darcie's eyes threatened to spill over. Her mother was right. But so far she had not been able to forgive the man responsible for their present circumstances. And it hurt to think the only man she'd ever felt such an attraction to was related to him.

"Please keep praying for me, Mama, because I am still struggling with it." She took a deep breath to collect herself.

"I'll go tell the boarders I'm sorry."

Her mother nodded and patted Darcie on the back. "Thank you. I love you, Darcie."

"I love you, too." Darcie returned her mother's hug, wishing she were more like her. With her gentle spirit, she had somehow forgiven the man who'd inflicted so much pain in their lives. Darcie wasn't sure she could ever forgive Douglas Harper the way her mother had.

She sighed and turned toward the dining room. She hoped she could make her apology to John Harper sound sincere. But when Darcie walked into the room, she discovered he had left the table. She wasn't sure if she felt relief or disappointment that she would have to wait until tomorrow to offer him her apology.

Apologizing to a sympathetic group of boarders presented no problem for her. She was sorry she'd ruined the nice meal her mother had planned for her. She grasped the back of the chair she'd vacated earlier and tried to smile at the three boarders still sitting at the table. "I am so sorry for my outburst earlier. I forgot my manners. I hope you will forgive me?"

"Oh, of course, Darcie, dear," Miss Olivia said.

"Think nothing of it," Mr. Mitchell added. "We understand." As her mother entered the dining room, he continued, "Mr. Harper was tired from his travels and asked us to tell you how delicious he found your meal, Mrs. Malone."

"Oh, I am sorry he didn't get a piece of cake. I'll be sure to save him a slice," she said.

Darcie knew from the look her mother shot her that she still expected her to apologize to John Harper; but, dear that she was, she said no more on the subject. Relieved for the moment, Darcie helped serve the cake. For the most part, the meal ended better than she deserved it to, considering how she'd disappointed her mother.

Feeling it was the very least she could do to show her mother she was truly sorry, Darcie insisted she leave the kitchen and dining room cleanup to her.

Her mother gave no protest. "Well, all right. I am a little tired tonight. Thank you, dear."

Determined the kitchen would be spotless when her mother came down the next morning, Darcie washed, dried, and swept, leaving no crumb behind. She even set the table for breakfast the next morning before she slipped up the back staircase to her room.

⁂

For more than an hour, John had paced the floor of the spacious room he'd rented earlier in the day. Finally he sat down at the writing desk to pen a letter to his parents. He couldn't telephone them long distance from here, and he didn't want to send a telegram. He didn't want people knowing any more about his business than was necessary. He wasn't sure what he was going to find out about his uncle, but from Darcie Malone's outburst earlier, he had a feeling it wouldn't be good.

He hadn't known what to do after Mrs. Malone and her daughter went into the kitchen. He'd felt uneasy sitting at the table with the other boarders and the silence that had suddenly fallen over the table. And he wasn't sure what to do now. Should he seek other accommodations or stay here?

Molly Malone was a wonderful cook. Her home was clean and comfortable, and he liked the woman. He shook his head. He'd sleep on it and decide tomorrow. Right now he needed to let his father know his only brother had died in prison.

John picked up his pen and started writing. He explained that his uncle had been in prison when he'd died and what he knew about it so far. He was honest with his father about not being sure how long the business of settling his uncle's estate would take.

How could he know how long he needed to uncover the depth of what he was just beginning to find out? And how could he voice his suspicions when that's all he had at the moment? Instead he promised he would stay as long as it took to settle everything—providing the people of Roswell didn't run him out of town before he could. But he didn't tell his father that part, either. It seemed enough for now that he had to tell him about his brother being incarcerated when he died. Perhaps by the time he had a reply from his father, he would have more of an idea of what settling his uncle's estate entailed. Slipping the letter into an envelope, he sealed and addressed it.

John stood up from the desk and stretched. It had been a long day, and he couldn't wait for the next one to arrive—just to get through his first day in Roswell. He didn't think he'd ever felt more unwelcome at any other time in his life.

He sauntered to the window and looked out before deciding to take a walk. Maybe the fresh night air would help him sleep soundly. He made sure he had the key to his room and the one Mrs. Malone had given him to the house, then put on his jacket and hat.

He heard murmurs coming from the back parlor; but no one was in the front parlor, and he was glad he didn't run into any of the boarders. He didn't want to feel he had to converse with anyone at the moment. He let himself out and turned in the direction of Main Street. The town was laid out well and the spring evening mild. He strolled up one side of the street and down the other. It appeared as if the dining rooms in several hotels were still open for business, but he was sure their fare couldn't hold a candle to Mrs. Malone's. Lights were out in the mercantile houses and other shops, but Emma's Café across from the sheriff's office appeared to be open.

He counted more than one drugstore in town and three blacksmith shops and two livery stables. The telephone office was still open, and he could see a young man working the switchboard through the window.

Several people were out and about and greeted him with a "Good evening."

By the time he turned back toward the Malone board inghouse, he was feeling a little better. Maybe he'd been too quick to judge the people of Roswell. And besides, surely, the whole town hadn't known his uncle.

❧

A plan had come to mind as Darcie was cleaning up. Once back in her room, she sat down at her desk and pulled out paper, pen, and ink. She quickly wrote a note of apology to John Harper.

> *Dear Mr. Harper,*
> *Please accept my apology for my rude outburst at the dinner table this evening. I should not have taken my dislike for your uncle out on you. I disappointed my mother greatly tonight, and for that I am truly sorry. Please do not hold my bad manners against her. I can assure you she taught me much better than that.*
>
> > *Sincerely,*
> > *Darcie Malone*

She was truly sorry about hurting her mother and could apologize sincerely for that. She folded the note and slipped it into an envelope and opened her door as quietly as she could. Making her way down the hall, she stopped outside John Harper's door and sent up a prayer that he wouldn't notice the note being slipped under his door—at least not until she was safely back in her own room.

The envelope slid under the door smoothly, and she let out a deep sigh of relief before turning and hurrying to her room. Darcie was aware she should have apologized in person and that her mother expected her to. But she hadn't been able to reconcile the way her pulse sped up at the thought of seeing him again with the anger she felt that anyone kin to Douglas Harper was sleeping in her home. She wasn't sure she could apologize to him any other way. At least not tonight.

After getting ready for bed, she picked up her Bible and settled in the window seat overlooking the front yard. The stars lighting the sky appeared close enough to reach out and touch. Darcie opened the Bible and tried to read her nightly devotional. But thoughts of the way she'd embarrassed her mother kept intruding. She tried to push them to the back of her mind, but the words on the page blurred through unshed tears. She slipped to her knees and bowed her head.

"Dear Father, please forgive me for upsetting Mama so. I am very sorry I hurt her. I was just shocked the nephew of that rat Douglas Harper had rented a room—"

Darcie bit her bottom lip and sighed as fresh tears formed and fell on her folded hands. "Father, I'm sorry," she whispered. "I know You would have me forgive my enemy. Mama seems to have. But I—I cannot get over the fact that Harper caused Papa's death. I'd pushed it to the back of my mind after finding out he died in prison. But now, with his nephew here—sleeping in this house—it's all come back, and I miss Papa so!"

She gave herself over to sobbing at the loss she felt anew. How could she ever forgive the man who'd caused her father's stroke? Because of him, her mother was working night and day! Yet her mother wanted her to forgive Harper and treat his nephew as she would any other boarder. Darcie wiped her eyes and sighed before continuing with her prayer.

"Father, I will try to be civil to John Harper, for Mama's sake. But please, please, if it be Your will—please let him decide to find another place to stay!"

How could she stand to have Douglas Harper's nephew— the last man she should ever be attracted to—staying in her home? Darcie shook her head. She didn't know. Only the Lord could help her. She finished her prayer. "Please help me to be more like Mama. In Jesus' name, amen."

❧

John let himself into the boardinghouse, nodded to Mr. Carlton and Mr. Mitchell, who were playing a game of chess in the front parlor, and headed up the stairs to his room. He unlocked the door and stepped inside to find an envelope on the floor.

Slipping off his jacket, he hung it on the hook beside the door and laid his hat on the table before turning up the gas light so he could read the letter. He was surprised and pleased to discover it was from Miss Darcie and even more so to find it was an apology. He read it a second time.

In the morning he'd have to assure her he in no way blamed her lapse of manners on her mother and that he accepted her apology. A light knock on the door had him wondering if it might be Darcie coming back to see if he'd found the note.

He opened the door, expecting her to be there. Instead it was Mrs. Malone standing with a tray that held a huge slice of chocolate cake on a plate and a cup of coffee. His mouth watered just looking at it.

"Mr. Harper, I felt so bad that you missed dessert because of my daughter's outburst. I hope you won't mind if I try to make it up to you now—"

"Oh, Mrs. Malone, please don't worry yourself about it. There's no need to make it up, but I certainly thank you for bringing this to me." With the note still in his hand, he took the tray from her.

"I'll collect the tray in the morning, and please be assured that Darcie will issue you an apology in the morning."

John smiled at the older woman. "Oh, but she already has."

"She has?"

"Yes, I was just reading her note of apology."

"She gave you a note instead of apologizing in person? No. That is not good enough. I'll have another talk—"

"Mrs. Malone, please don't. I went out for a walk and just returned. She probably would have told me in person had I been here. The note was slipped under my door while I was out."

Darcie's mother shook her head. "Still—"

"It's a nice note, Mrs. Malone. And of course I accept her apology." John didn't want her to force her daughter into a face-to-face apology. After seeing her distress this evening at the table, he was surprised even to receive the note.

"Well, I—please accept mine, also. I'm afraid your first night here wasn't—"

"The meal was delicious. While I was out walking, I was thankful for such a nice place to stay while I'm here. I've never been particularly fond of hotels. And to come back to a piece of that delicious-looking cake—I'll have to thank Mr. Griffin for steering me in your direction."

He seemed to have assured Mrs. Malone to her satisfaction because she smiled and shook her head. "Thank you, Mr. Harper. I will let you enjoy your dessert. Thank you for letting me know Darcie did apologize, even if it wasn't in the way I would have liked."

"You are welcome." John inclined his head toward the tray in his hands. "And thank you."

Darcie's mother nodded and turned to leave. "Good night, Mr. Harper."

"Good night, Mrs. Malone."

She closed the door behind her, and John carried the tray over to the small table in front of the window. He pulled out one of the two chairs and sat down to enjoy the piece of cake. He closed his eyes as he took his first bite. It was as scrumptious as it looked and smelled. No wonder it was a favorite of the other boarders. He sipped the coffee, then leaned back in his chair. Maybe his stay here would turn out better than he first thought. He hoped it would. He prayed it would.

four

Darcie was up bright and early the next morning, a little nervous about starting her new position. She dressed with care and chose a navy blue skirt and a crisp white blouse. She took extra time with her hair, pulling it into the fashionable psyche knot. When she was satisfied she looked professional, she hurried downstairs to help her mother get breakfast ready for the boarders.

The first meal of the day was not a formal one, but it was always large. Her mother prepared quite an array of items and set them out on the sideboard in the dining room so her boarders could help themselves whenever they came down.

Her mother greeted her with her usual cheery, "Good morning, dear."

"Good morning, Mama. I hope your day is an easy one." She kissed the cheek her mother turned to her as she was sliding flapjacks onto a plate.

"Thank you, Darcie. I hope for the same for you. And thank you for writing Mr. Harper that note of apology, though I wish you'd apologized to him in person—"

"He's been down already?"

"No, dear. Not that I know of. I felt bad that he'd missed dessert last night and took him a piece of cake—he told me then. He'd just come back from a walk and found your note."

"Oh. Well—"

"He appeared to be quite satisfied by it, and that is the main thing. He seems a nice young man and nothing like his uncle, Darcie." She added the last pancake to the pile and handed the plate to Darcie. "We need to—"

"I know. Get these to the dining room." Darcie took the platter from her mother, then glanced back on her way out of the kitchen and saw the look on her mother's face.

"Darcie, you know full well that is not what I was talking about."

"I know. I'm sorry, Mama. I will try." And she promised herself she would try to be civil to the man for her mother's sake.

"Thank you, dear. That is all I'm asking you to do."

Darcie breathed a sigh of relief as she entered the dining room and added the platter to the rest of the fare on the sideboard. Along with the pancakes were butter and warmed syrup, bacon and sausage, and scrambled eggs. A basket of sweet rolls and biscuits and an assortment of jellies completed the choices. As she fixed her own plate, she was sure no other boardinghouse in town put on the kind of spread her mother did. Darcie sighed and shook her head. If only her mother didn't have to work so hard.

She heard footsteps on the stairs and some of the boarders greeting each other, and she returned to the kitchen to eat her breakfast there as she did most mornings. She always tried to help her mother by washing up some of the cookware before heading off to work, but this morning she had the added incentive of not having to face John Harper.

"Have a good day, dear," her mother said as she took off her apron and prepared to join her guests.

"You, too, Mama. If you need anything from downtown, just telephone me."

Her mother nodded as she went through the door. Darcie heard her greet the boarders with her customary, "Good morning! I hope you all rested well?"

She could hear the murmur of voices assuring her mother they had indeed slept very well. But it was John Harper's voice that started her pulse racing and her temper rising as he told her mother he'd never slept better.

How dare he sleep so well under this roof? But of even more concern to her was how her heart could beat so fast at the sound of his voice from the other room! No longer hungry, she made quick work of washing her dishes and the cooking pans and utensils so her mother wouldn't have to, all the while trying desperately to get her mind off Douglas Harper's nephew.

Drying her hands on the dish towel, Darcie took a quick look in the mirror by the back door to make sure she looked presentable for her first day as head operator. Then she hurried out the door and around the side yard to the walk that would take her to Main Street. Relieved she hadn't run into any of the boarders—one in particular—she walked as fast as she could until she was out of sight of the house. She'd be glad to get to work.

❧

John had dreaded coming downstairs and having breakfast with everyone after last night; but by the time he'd finished Mrs. Malone's delicious pancakes, he was even more thankful Elmer Griffin had told him about this place. The other boarders had warmed up to him after taking their cue from their landlady, who had gone out of her way to make him feel welcome. He knew that even though her daughter hadn't made an appearance at the table, he wasn't going to seek lodging anywhere else—notwithstanding the fact he was fairly sure Miss Darcie Malone would prefer it that way.

Surely she wouldn't decide to avoid meals altogether—and he doubted her mother would let her get away with that should she try. He was hoping to get a glimpse of her beautiful red hair and flashing blue-green eyes before the day was out.

He left the boardinghouse with Mr. Carlton and Mr. Mitchell and was glad for their company as they headed toward Main Street. He bid them good-bye and sauntered the few blocks to his uncle's bank, but he realized everyone still didn't welcome him. Several people slowed down their stroll past the bank, watching him unlock the door. When he tipped his hat toward them and wished them a good morning, they scattered, with frowns on their brows. Maybe some of them owed his uncle money, and as Elmer Griffin had warned him, they weren't going to be welcoming. Of course most of these people didn't even know who he was yet, but it didn't appear that any of them wanted to find out.

John's good mood of the morning suddenly dissipated as he realized the only place he might feel comfortable was at Molly Malone's—and probably only if Darcie wasn't around. He sighed and opened the dusty shutters over the windows. He sneezed then and realized he'd need to hire someone to come in to clean. He'd ask Mrs. Malone about that this evening.

As he entered his uncle's office, it occurred to him that Douglas Harper must have been a man who wanted to control his surroundings. The office was situated so he could see everything going on in the bank. Sitting in the massive chair, John pulled the pile of folders he'd left in the middle of the desk toward him.

By midmorning, he'd barely made a dent in the first batch of paperwork he'd chosen to review. At first it appeared his uncle kept detailed records, but on closer inspection many seemed incomplete. His uncle's handwriting was appalling and nearly impossible to decipher.

John was relieved to see Elmer Griffin when he showed

up around eleven as promised. His uncle had apparently not been above board in all his business dealings, and John realized he needed help in dealing with it.

He stood and shook Elmer's hand. "I'm glad you didn't change your mind about coming. I'm having trouble reading my uncle's handwriting."

"I'm fortunate I'm at a point in life where I can take only cases that interest me. Not many do. So I have nothing on my docket now, and you seem like a nice sort and nothing like your uncle. Let me see what you have." He reached for the pile of papers John pushed across the desk to him.

"I'd be glad of any help you give me, sir. I hope you can decipher my uncle's script better than I can."

Elmer pushed his spectacles up on his nose and peered at the top page. He shook his head. "We have our work cut out for us, son."

John nodded. "Yes, I'm afraid we do."

❧

Mr. McQuillen introduced Darcie as the new head operator and supervisor first thing that morning. She was pleased no one seemed upset. In fact, her coworkers appeared genuinely happy for her. She accepted their congratulations and started her first day in her new position with the best intentions of being a wonderful example to the other operators, just as Beth had been to her.

But it didn't take long for those good intentions to fall by the wayside. Hard as she was trying not to think about John Harper when she arrived at work, it soon became obvious she wasn't succeeding.

When the Winslows' line lit up, she smiled as she put the line pin into the socket. She hadn't talked to her best friend in several days. It was always good to hear from her. "Good morning, Beth. Who can I connect you to?"

"Darcie, I want to talk to you! When were you going to tell me the news?"

Darcie's heart jumped in her chest. Who told Beth about Harper's nephew being in town? "Why, Beth, I didn't think word traveled that fast in this town. He only got here yesterday."

"He who?"

"John—" Darcie stopped midsentence. Did Beth not know? "What news are we talking about, Beth?"

Beth giggled on the other end of the line. "Right now we appear to be talking about John someone, and I can't wait to find out who he is. But I was talking about your promotion."

"Oh, I'm sorry. I meant to telephone you last night."

"It's all right. I couldn't wait to congratulate you! I put in a good word for you with Mr. McQuillen, and I was so hoping you would get the promotion."

"Thank you, Beth. I'll never be as good a supervisor as you, but I'll try."

"You'll do fine. Now—who is this John person?"

Beth took a deep breath. "He is John Harper. Mama's new boarder."

"Oh, I'm glad she has a new one—"

Darcie shook her head. "Not this one, Beth."

"Oh? Why not?"

"H-a-r-p-e-r. As in the nephew of Douglas Harper."

"Ohh. Darcie, I am so sorry. How did that happen? I can't believe your mother rented a—"

"She didn't know." Darcie was quick to take up for her mother. How could she have blamed her? She hadn't made the connection to Douglas Harper, either.

"What did your mother say when she found out who he was? And what is he like?" Beth shot off the questions. "And what did she do? Tell him to get out?"

I wish. Several lines lit up at the same time, and much as Darcie wanted to answer Beth's questions, she had to cut their conversation short. "Beth, it's getting busy. I—"

"I understand. I'm coming into town later. Ring me through to Emma's—and plan to have afternoon tea at her place soon's you get off work, so you can fill us in."

"All right." Darcie connected Beth's line to Emma's Café. She was glad she didn't have to go into it here at work but would have a chance to talk to Beth later. She hurried to plug in another line. "Number, please?"

"Darcie, it's Alma Burton. Could you ring me through to Doc's, please? I need to talk to Myrtle."

"Right away, Mrs. Alma." Darcie plugged Alma Burton's line into Doc Bradshaw's socket. Alma Burton was a favorite of everyone who worked the switchboards. She hoped nothing was wrong with the older woman; her voice sounded odd. Alma had been lonesome since the death of her husband several years before, and she often rang through to the telephone office to catch up on news around town. Darcie was happy to oblige when she could, but now that she was head operator, she'd have to be more cautious.

The operators were supposed to be careful about carrying on personal conversations while at work, but everyone seemed to make an exception for Mrs. Burton. Besides, it was hard to keep everything on a professional level when most of the residents looked to the telephone operators to find out what was going on in town.

Of course if an emergency occurred, all rules were suspended. Then the operators were expected to get word out to the Roswell Telephone and Manufacturing Company's customers. According to Beth, hardly any rules existed out here in the West compared to the Bell Telephone Company back East where she'd been trained. Darcie had a feeling she would never have made head operator back East. She probably wouldn't have even made it as a regular operator.

She was trying hard not to start any gossip. So throughout the day, she managed to stop short of shouting to one and all that Douglas Harper's nephew was back in town to settle the man's estate. What would that mean to so many in Roswell who'd done business with his bank? And shouldn't she be warning them?

Darcie finally convinced herself it was indeed her duty and mentioned it to Liddy McAllister when she rang in to put in a call to Emma's Café. Harper had been awful to Liddy when she was a young widow expecting her first child. She was thankful Cal McAllister had come along and taken care of Harper for her, but if he hadn't been around, the banker probably would have ended up with Liddy's land.

"Oh, Darcie. Do you suppose he's going to cause as many problems as Douglas did?"

"I certainly hope not, Liddy, but I don't know."

"I pray he is nothing like his uncle. How did he—?"

"Liddy, I have to go." Darcie watched as one line and then three more lit up. It was promising to be a busy day, which was probably for the best. "I'm going to meet Beth at Em's for tea about four o'clock," she said hurriedly. "If you can, try to come in then, too. I'll fill you in then."

"I'll be there," Liddy said right before the connection was broken.

It was half an hour later before they had a lull. Darcie glanced over at Jessica Landry, one of the other operators on duty, and blew out a deep breath.

Jessica smiled at her. "Darcie, I haven't meant to listen in, but did I hear you mention earlier that Douglas Harper's nephew is in town?"

"Yes, you did."

"Oh, dear. I hope that doesn't mean trouble."

"So do I. Especially as he is staying at my mother's boardinghouse." Darcie understood Jessica's sharp intake of breath. "Mother says we can't hold his uncle's sins against him. I know she's right, but—"

"That doesn't make things easy for you, does it?"

Red lights lit up on Darcie's switchboard once more. She saw the same thing happening on Jessica's board and only had time to shrug at the other woman before they both went back to work.

When she heard Jessica mention to several customers that Douglas Harper's nephew was in town, she couldn't bring herself to reprimand her. After all, the other girl had overheard Darcie mentioning it to Liddy. Besides, she truly felt deep down that people needed to know John Harper was in town and there to settle his uncle's estate.

❧

By four o'clock, Darcie was more than ready for a cup of tea. Her three dear friends were waiting for her at a corner table at Emma's. Emma Johnson was the proprietor of the café and the wife of one of the town's deputies, Matt Johnson. She was expecting a child in a few months and had never looked prettier. Liddy and Emma had been friends for a long time, and in the last few years, they'd become good friends with newly married Beth Winslow and Darcie. They'd shared heartaches and joys with one another, and Darcie felt blessed to have each one in her life.

Now the other women barely waited for Darcie to take a seat before they began to quiz her.

"Is it true Harper's nephew is in town, Beth?" Emma asked as she poured her a cup of tea.

"Yes, it is true, Em."

Emma groaned. "I thought we'd heard the last of Douglas Harper when he died in prison."

"So did I." Darcie took a sip from her cup.

"What do you think his nephew is doing here?" Emma asked.

"I don't know, Em. He says he's here to settle his uncle's estate."

"Humph! I hope that doesn't mean more trouble for the citizens of Roswell," Emma said.

"So do I," Beth added.

Darcie had to tell them. "He's also staying at the boarding-house."

"At your boardinghouse?" Emma questioned.

Darcie nodded. "Mother didn't know he was related to Douglas Harper when she rented a room to him, but she won't tell him to find another place."

"Oh, dear. How do you feel about that?"

Before or after I found out who he was? "Upset." *Especially as I can't quit thinking about how handsome he is or how nice he seems to be.*

"I can understand that. I feel that way just knowing he's in town," Emma said.

Darcie nodded. "I know. But Mother says we can't hold him accountable for his uncle's actions."

"She's right, you know," Liddy said. "But it's very hard, isn't it?"

"Very hard."

"What is he like, Darcie?" Beth asked.

"Well, he has nice manners and—" The bell over the café

door jingled then, and Darcie looked up to see the topic of their conversation walk in the door with Elmer Griffin. When he spotted her, he smiled and tipped his hat in her direction before sitting down at a table on the other side of the room.

"And there he is," she whispered, hoping no one could see the slight tremble of her fingers as she picked up her teacup and took a sip to try to hide her reaction to the man.

"That's him?" Liddy whispered back.

Darcie nodded over the rim of her cup. He certainly did look handsome in his black Barrington worsted suit.

"Oh, dear," Beth said. "He doesn't look anything like his uncle."

"No. He doesn't, does he?" Liddy said. "Let's hope he's as different from the man as he looks."

Emma glanced at John Harper and nodded. "We can hope. And time will tell, I suppose."

Darcie looked up to find Beth's thoughtful gaze on her. She only hoped her best friend couldn't see what a turmoil her emotions were in.

Beth took a sip of tea and nodded. "Yes, only time will tell."

five

John was glad Darcie was at the dinner table that night. He'd found it hard to get her out of his mind after running into her at the restaurant that afternoon. She'd left Emma's Café before he and Elmer had, and he'd hoped she wouldn't go into hiding once she got home. She looked lovely tonight. She'd changed into a pretty yellow dress that made her hair seem even brighter than usual.

Tonight's meal was much more pleasant than the previous night's had been. When he walked in the front door, he caught the aroma of the rich stew Mrs. Malone had made from the leftover beef, and his stomach started to growl. With it, she served corn bread and biscuits that melted in John's mouth.

But it wasn't the food that made the evening for John, good as it was. It was the fact that Darcie was civil to him, and everyone else at the table seemed amiable, too, as if taking their cue from her and her mother. He enjoyed listening to the conversation taking place around him.

"How did your first day as head operator go, Darcie?" Miss Waterford asked.

"I think I will have to grow into the job, Miss Olivia," Darcie answered. "I'm sure I'll never be as good a manager as Beth was, but I will try."

"How is Beth enjoying married life?" the other woman asked. "Have you seen her lately?"

Darcie smiled and nodded. "I saw her this afternoon. She

47

is quite happy and not missing the telephone office at all."

"That's good," Miss Waterford replied.

"I think marriage agrees with her. She fairly glows from taking care of Jeb and the children. I'm so glad she and Jeb fell in love and can provide a family for his brother's children."

"I am so happy for them," Mrs. Malone said as she dished up apple cobbler for dessert. "The four of them make a beautiful family."

Mr. Carlton took a bite. "Mmm. This cobbler is delicious, Mrs. Malone."

"Thank you. The apples came from Beth and Jeb's orchard. The Winslow apples won first place at the fair last year. These are some of the last Beth brought us. I stored them in the cellar."

"Well, they deserved to win if they held up this long."

"Everything was wonderful, Mrs. Malone," John said.

"Thank you." She smiled. "I enjoy putting a good meal on the table."

"Well, that you do—each and every day," Mr. Mitchell said.

"Mama, have you talked to Alma Burton lately?"

John enjoyed the excuse to look at Darcie without appearing to be staring at her.

"Not in the last few days, dear. Why?"

"She rang through to talk to Doc today and didn't sound like herself. I hope she's all right."

Mrs. Malone's face clouded with concern. "So do I. I'll check on her tomorrow."

Darcie nodded. "Good. I worry about her."

"She needs to sell that house of hers and move in here. She's alone too much, and that isn't good for a body," Miss Waterford added.

"I think she hates to give up her home. She and her husband

were very happy there, but I worry it's too much for her to keep up with, too." Mrs. Malone sighed.

"You know, she probably would enjoy living here if we could get her to try it," Darcie said. "I think she must get awful lonesome living by herself."

John was touched by their concern for their friend. As mother and daughter cleared the table and he excused himself from the room, he found himself wishing he could be included in the circle of people they cared about.

He returned from his nightly walk and went upstairs to his room; only then did he realize no one had asked about what he was doing in regard to his uncle's business. Was it because they didn't care or didn't want to know—or were afraid to find out?

The more he delved into his uncle's papers, the surer he was that it was one of the latter two possibilities. John sighed deeply. Well, they weren't alone in their fears. The more he found out about Douglas Harper's business practices, the more he feared what was to come. Soon he would have to talk to people in this town to find out if what he suspected about his uncle was true. He'd been praying he was wrong, but nothing he could find pointed in that direction. Nothing.

He couldn't change the past or what his uncle might have done to hurt the good people of Roswell. He could only hope to try to ease some of the pain, especially for the Malone family. Darcie must have had a reason for reacting so strongly that first night when she found out he was Douglas Harper's nephew. But he didn't know how to ask about it in a way that wouldn't upset her and her mother again.

John let out a deep breath and opened his Bible. He hoped that somehow, in researching his uncle's papers, he'd run across an explanation concerning Darcie's family. In the meantime, he'd gain strength from reading God's Word and go to Him in prayer for help in making things right. No matter how difficult that became or how long it took, he meant to keep looking to the Lord for guidance.

❧

The next few days were a mixture of frustration and—something else Darcie couldn't quite name. Frustration because she couldn't stop her heart from beating faster each time she saw John Harper. Frustration because she found herself looking forward to seeing him each evening, then suddenly dreading it as she reminded herself he was the nephew of Douglas Harper—and the last person in the world she should be attracted to.

But charmed by him she was—and fighting it with every fiber of her being. Darcie entered the dining room and hurried toward the kitchen to help her mother. She tried to ignore her racing pulse as she recognized the deep timbre of his voice talking to one of the boarders in the front parlor. She released a deep breath when she stepped into the kitchen and placed her hand over her heart.

Her mother glanced up from the platter she was filling with fried chicken. "Darcie, dear, are you all right? You look a little flushed."

Darcie avoided meeting her mother's eyes. Instead she grabbed the bowls of mashed potatoes and cream gravy to carry to the dining room. "I'm fine, Mama. I've felt a bit rushed all day."

"Well, there's no hurry here, dear. I'm sure not one of our boarders will up and leave if supper is a little late getting to the table." She shed her apron and picked up the chicken platter.

"You're right about that." Darcie chuckled and shook her

head. "They all know there isn't a better boardinghouse in town than Molly Malone's." She managed to give her mother a bright smile as they took the food to the dining room.

Her mother crossed to the hall and called her boarders to the table. Darcie greeted them as a group while they took their seats.

As he'd done each night since he'd come to her mother's establishment, John Harper held Darcie's chair for her and made sure she was comfortable before he took his seat. He had impeccable manners, which seemed to have a good influence on the other two gentlemen boarders. Darcie smiled as she watched Mr. Carlton extend the same courtesy to her mother while Mr. Mitchell did the same for Miss Olivia. The two men had been taking turns seating the two older women since Mr. Harper had started doing so his first night at the table.

After Mr. Carlton said the blessing, her mother passed the platters and bowls around the table while the others served themselves. When the dishes reached Darcie's end of the table, she handed them to John Harper. He always smiled when he thanked her, which made her catch her breath for a second, much to her exasperation. For then she sounded breathless as she answered, "You are welcome."

She was thankful for the temporary lull in conversation as everyone began to eat. She wondered if there was any way to persuade her mother to change the seating arrangements so she wasn't sitting so close to the man. Somehow she didn't think so. She was sure her mother would consider it rude, and Darcie knew it would be. But it was getting increasingly hard to ignore the way this man made her feel. He was so charming—so—

She took a sip of water and reminded herself his uncle had

been engaging, too, when it suited his purpose. Perhaps that's what this man was doing. Her heart twisted in her chest at the thought he might be like his uncle.

"Darcie? Dear?"

Concern in her mother's voice brought Darcie out of her reverie. "I'm sorry, Mama. What were you saying?"

"I talked to Alma today. You were right to wonder about her health. She's not been feeling herself and went to Doc for a checkup." Her mother shook her head.

"What's wrong?" Darcie hoped it was nothing serious.

"It appears she's just getting over the influenza. Doc says she should have come to him earlier, and he doesn't want her to stay by herself until she's completely recovered."

"Oh, dear. What is she going to do?" Miss Olivia asked.

"I've convinced her to come stay here with us until she gets totally well."

"Influenza?" Mr. Carlton asked. "Isn't that contagious?"

"I talked to Doc about that, too. He says she weathered the worst of it by herself. She isn't contagious now," her mother reassured him. "We just feel it would be better for her to stay here so I can see she eats right and continues to recover."

"Well, I suppose that does make sense," Mr. Mitchell said.

"Of course it does," said Miss Olivia. "I'm sure it will do her good to be around other people, too. When will she be arriving?"

"Tomorrow. I'll prepare a room for her tonight—"

"If you need assistance getting her here, I'll be glad to help," John Harper said.

There he goes again, Darcie thought. *Being nice and sweet to my mother. Is it genuine, or is it an act?* She wished she knew.

"Why, Mr. Harper, how nice of you to offer. Thank you so much. But Doc said he would bring her over."

"I'll help get her room ready, Mama," Darcie said. "Do you think we can convince her to stay once she's better? I hate the thought of her being sick and alone. If she goes back, it could happen again."

"I know. And I'm hoping she'll decide to sell her house and stay with us." Her mother smiled, then gazed around the table. "Mrs. Alma Burton is like family to Darcie and me. I hope you will help us make her feel at home here."

Darcie stifled a chuckle at her mother's directness. Put that way, they couldn't do much but agree.

"Of course, of course," Mr. Mitchell said, nodding.

"We'll do our best," Mr. Carlton said.

"Thank you," her mother said. "I feel much relieved that she'll be staying with us, and I intend to do all I can to convince her to stay."

"I'll strive to make her feel as welcome as you've made me feel, Molly," Miss Olivia assured her. "I'm sure it won't take long for her to decide to bask in your gentle care."

"Thank you for those kind words, Olivia. And thank you all for your support and loyalty," her mother added.

Once dinner was over, Darcie took over cleaning up the dining room and kitchen while her mother went upstairs to ready the room for Mrs. Alma. She suspected Miss Olivia would be keeping her mother company. She seemed glad they would have another woman boarder. Her mother had told her that sometimes Miss Olivia followed her around while she worked, talking the whole way. Darcie chuckled. She wondered how Mrs. Alma would take to Miss Olivia. And how they would all take to Mrs. Alma. She was a character and would liven up the dinner table once they got her on the road to recovery.

Mr. Carlton and Mr. Mitchell were already setting up their usual game of chess in the front parlor by the time she had cleared the table, and she supposed John had gone for his customary walk. As she plunged her hands in the hot water to wash the dishes, Darcie grudgingly admitted it had been nice of him to offer to help, and she could tell her mother had appreciated it. Could he be nothing like his uncle? Much as Darcie wished that to be true, she was afraid to hope it was. And what did it matter anyway? There was no way she could let herself care about someone related to the man she held accountable for her father's death. No way. No matter how fast her pulse raced at the sight of him.

After she'd dried the last dish and set the dining room table for the next morning, she went upstairs to see if she could help her mother. Much to Darcie's surprise, she found her mother directing John Harper on where to place a small settee that had been brought down from the attic.

"There—just center it in front of the window, please, John," her mother was saying.

"Oh, that looks very nice," Miss Olivia said from across the room.

John straightened the cream-colored settee and backed up. "It does look very nice there, Mrs. Malone. Much better than at the end of the bed, in my opinion."

Darcie noticed the bed had been moved, too. "Mama, I would have helped. Why didn't you call me?"

Her mother motioned her into the room. "I would have, dear. But Mr. Harper happened by before he went for a walk and kindly offered. His help has been invaluable, too."

Darcie looked around. Everything in the room seemed to be in a different spot. "I can see you've kept him busy."

Her mother chuckled and turned to John. "Yes, I have. Thank you so much."

"I was glad to help. Please feel free to call on me anytime.

My mother loves to move furniture around, and my father hates to." He grinned. "Guess who gets to help her?"

"No wonder your suggestions were so helpful. Your mother sounds like a woman after my own heart."

"You do remind me of her. I think that's why I'm so happy to be staying here."

"Why, what a nice thing to say, John."

John nodded and grinned. "I meant it."

"I've taken up enough of your time tonight. You go on ahead with your walk."

"Are you sure everything is where you want it?"

"I think the room looks lovely, don't you, Darcie?"

Darcie had thought it was fine the way it was before, but it did look more inviting like this. The settee, a table, and a matching chair had been grouped closer to the fireplace to form a nice sitting area for Mrs. Alma. The four-poster bed had been turned to face the window. And another chair had been placed beside a bedside table. It seemed cozy, and she was sure Mrs. Alma would enjoy it. And she did appreciate John Harper's helping her mother, despite the fact she didn't want to feel beholden to him in any way.

"It looks wonderful, Mama. I'm sure Mrs. Alma is going to love it." She paused a moment before turning to John. "Thank you for helping my mother, Mr. Harper."

He smiled. "Glad to do it." He nodded to her mother. "Call on me anytime, Mrs. Malone. If the furniture is as you want it and you're sure you no longer need my help, I'll go for my walk now."

"You go on. I think Alma will be happy here. Thank you again."

"You're welcome." He paused at the door and turned back. "Good evening, ladies."

John looked in on the chess game for a few minutes before starting out. Mr. Carlton was winning at the moment, but Mr. Mitchell assured John he'd be ahead before long. Chuckling at the two men's banter, John bid them good evening, too, and headed toward Main Street.

All in all it had been a pretty good night. He was glad he'd been able to help Mrs. Malone, even though he could tell Darcie wasn't thrilled about it. She still wasn't happy about his staying in her home, but he was sure that, for her mother's sake, she would continue to try to make the best of it. John admired her greatly for putting her mother's wishes before her own.

He must find out the truth about what his uncle had done to hurt the Malones. Perhaps not yet. But soon he had to know.

six

Mrs. Alma Burton moved to the boardinghouse the next day, and Darcie and her mother were much relieved to have her there. Although only in her sixties, her illness had taken a toll and seemed to have aged her, and they were determined to help her return to the feisty woman they loved.

Her mother seated her directly across from John and on Darcie's left side. It was Darcie's job to make sure the older woman ate enough. The other boarders tried to make her feel welcome, and Mrs. Alma perked up a little with their attention.

Her soft, graying hair was done up in a bun and her blue eyes bright as she listened to the conversations at the table. Darcie knew her well enough to know Mrs. Alma loved people and little escaped her notice. She was acquainted with the older boarders as she'd taken a Sunday meal with the Malones from time to time, so it seemed natural for her to study John.

Darcie was sure she'd have something to say about him once he was out of earshot. Once the meal was over and the gentlemen left the room, Mrs. Alma scorned the suggestion that her mother help her upstairs; instead she insisted on staying downstairs.

❧

Miss Olivia was delighted to have Alma Burton in the house and offered to show her the parlors and help her upstairs if she tired out.

"Thank you, Olivia, but I've been coming to the Malone home since before it was a boardinghouse. I know where the parlors are. And if I should need help getting upstairs, I'll be sure to ask," she said matter-of-factly.

Miss Olivia appeared about to cry. "Oh, I'm sorry, Mrs. Alma. I was just trying—"

"To be nice, I know. I understand, and I do thank you." Mrs. Alma nodded. "Guess I'm too independent at times. I didn't mean to hurt your feelings. I'll come sit a spell in the parlor with you."

Mollified, Miss Olivia quickly agreed.

"Would you like me to bring down your knitting, Alma?" Darcie's mother asked. Anyone acquainted with Alma Burton knew she liked to keep her hands busy with quilting, knitting, or tatting.

"I'll be glad to go get it for you," Miss Olivia offered.

This time Mrs. Alma agreed. "That would be good of you."

"I'll run upstairs and then meet you in the front parlor." Miss Olivia smiled sweetly at the older woman and hurried up the stairs.

"She's a nice woman, Alma. She just gets a little lonesome at times and needs some woman talk."

"I can see that, Molly. That's why you asked me to stay—to give your ear a break?" She smiled. Then, sure as Darcie had been expecting her to, she brought up John Harper. "Or are you trying to fix me up with that handsome new boarder of yours? He's a little young for me, you know. But he'd be just right for Darcie."

"Mrs. Alma!" Darcie could feel the heat rising in her cheeks and was thankful no other boarders were left at the table, especially John.

Her mother shook her head at her good friend. "Alma Burton, what are we going do with you?"

"Still and all, it's a thought," Mrs. Alma said, chuckling as she headed toward the front parlor.

And it was a thought so outrageous even Darcie had to chuckle as she began to clear the table. It might take awhile for the boarders to get used to the older woman, but she had a heart of gold and wouldn't intentionally hurt anyone. She just had a habit of saying what she thought. But she was way off in her thinking tonight. John Harper would be the last man her mother would try to fix her up with. The very last one

❧

The next day was Sunday, and John did as he would at home. After Mrs. Malone's self-serve breakfast on the sideboard—she had made it clear she felt her place was in the Lord's house on Sunday—he put on the coat to his best suit, then set out for church.

He'd asked Elmer about churches in town and was pleased to find one was located only a few blocks from the boarding-house. He enjoyed the brisk walk to the small white building. The church was not as large as the one he attended at home, but it didn't matter. It felt good to sing God's praise and hear a message from His Word. Of course, several people turned their heads when they saw him, while others nudged the person they were sitting next to and whispered. He had no doubt he was the topic of conversation and that whatever was being said about him wasn't favorable.

Deep down he sensed they weren't reacting to him person-ally; they didn't even know him. But they'd known his uncle, and because of him and his actions, they didn't trust John.

He couldn't blame them. He just wished he didn't have to deal with it. But he did—not only for his sake, but also for the sake of his family's name. So he would do the best he could to bring honor back to his family name in the town.

John forced his attention back to the sermon and the message of 2 Timothy about fighting a good fight, staying the course, and keeping the faith. It was a lesson he needed to hear. Perhaps God was encouraging him to stay here and do what was needed. And he would—with His help.

Near the end of the service, he spotted Darcie, her mother, and Alma Burton in a pew a few rows in front of him. He couldn't explain the pleasure he felt seeing them there. Even though they were barely more than acquaintances, he suddenly felt as if he'd found long lost friends. Even if they were suspicious of his actions because of his uncle, at least they were civil to him.

Once the closing prayer was said, he stepped into the aisle. He planned to wait for the Malones and walk out with them. But he couldn't help hearing what people up the aisle from him were saying.

"Can you believe it? Douglas Harper's nephew is here in our church. How does he have the nerve?" one woman whispered loudly.

"Wonder what he's up to?" the woman at her side asked.

"Probably here to collect the debts owed to his uncle."

"Humph! Well, he'd better not come around my house. Harold will pull out his shotgun!"

With that, they swept past him and down the aisle.

John took a deep breath. It seemed each day, even on Sunday, he was to be reminded of how much the townspeople disliked Douglas Harper. He shook his head in bewilderment. How his uncle could have been so opposite from his father was beyond him. It was becoming obvious to him that no two brothers could be any more different.

He turned to go. He wasn't sure he was good company right now. Distracted, he almost missed the minister's greeting.

"Mr. Harper, isn't it?" The man held out his hand.

"Yes. John Harper," he said, shaking the older man's hand.

"I'm Minister Turley. Welcome to Roswell."

Taken aback by the sincerity in the minister's voice, John could only say, "Thank you." But he felt compelled to add, "I'm Douglas Harper's nephew."

Minister Turley nodded. "Yes, I thought so. I heard you were in town."

"Did he attend church here?"

The minister shook his head. "No. I don't know that Harper attended any church regularly."

John shrugged. "I didn't know my uncle well at all—and I—"

"I understand, son." Minister Turley clapped his hand to his shoulder. "I think you have a hard job ahead of you. But the fact you're here today tells me you know Whom to turn to when life gets tough."

"I do." John smiled at the man and felt connected by their mutual faith in God.

"I look forward to seeing you next week," Minister Turley said.

"I'll be here." His faith strengthened by Minister Turley's lesson and welcome, John changed his mind about leaving right away. He walked down the church steps and stood under a huge cottonwood to wait for the Malone women and Mrs. Burton.

He watched the minister greet them. Darcie's smile was contagious as she responded to something the minister said to her, and John wished she'd smile at him that way, just once. Well, no. To be honest, he wished she'd smile at him like that all the time. But somehow the shine in her eyes seemed to dim when she caught sight of him, and he didn't know how to change it. For the first time in his life, he wished his last name was anything but Harper.

"John!" Mrs. Malone said as they strolled toward him. "If I'd known you were coming to church, we'd have waited and walked with you."

"I'd have been honored to escort you ladies to church. I hope you'll let me see you back home?"

"Of course," Mrs. Malone said, falling in step beside Mrs. Burton and leaving Darcie no choice but to walk beside him.

"How did you like Minister Turley's sermon today?" Mrs. Malone asked.

"He's a very good preacher. I look forward to hearing him again." *And, Lord, I'll try to keep my mind on the message instead of worrying about what everyone is saying about me.*

Darcie looked as fresh as the spring day in her green-and-white striped dress. In the sunlight, her eyes seemed even greener. Her auburn hair was pulled on top of her head and topped by a hat that matched her dress. John couldn't deny he was attracted to this woman—even though he was probably the last man on earth she'd ever let court her.

Court her? Now where did that come from? He was here to settle his uncle's estate. His family expected him home as soon as he'd finished. He had no business thinking of courting Miss Darcie Malone. None at all.

"Mr. Harper?"

"I'm sorry, Mrs. Malone. I must have been woolgathering—" John paused. No way could he tell her he was thinking about her daughter.

"You have spring fever," Mrs. Burton said all of a sudden, saving him from having to finish his sentence.

"Beg pardon?"

"You know, a young man's fancy turns to love in the spring."

"No, ma'am, I didn't know that." He felt his face grow warm, then glanced at Darcie to see a soft pink color rising on her cheeks.

"Alma!" Mrs. Malone chuckled and shook her head. "Don't mind Mrs. Burton, John. She's just teasing you. I was asking if you like ice cream."

"Oh, yes, ma'am, I do."

"Good. I hope you won't mind taking a turn cranking our churn today. It's such a beautiful warm day—I think ice cream will make a good dessert. You men can take care of that while Darcie and I set out Sunday dinner."

"I'd be glad to help." He'd been debating whether or not to look through some of his uncle's papers he'd brought home the night before, but making ice cream sounded a lot more relaxing.

"I think I'd like some ice cream, too," Mrs. Burton said.

"I was hoping you'd say that, Alma. Doc says we need to fatten you up a little. I thought your favorite dessert might help."

ã

As Darcie helped her mother set out the meal, she was keenly aware of the men outside the back door, cranking the ice cream freezer. Well, of John Harper in particular. He was always eager to lend a hand if asked. In truth, he seemed nothing at all like his uncle, but still Darcie didn't trust him. Couldn't let herself even begin to.

When the telephone rang four quick rings and one long one for their special ring, she hurried to answer it. They didn't get many calls this time of day on Sunday.

"Darcie?"

"Beth! How good to hear from you. Have you finished your dinner already?" She and Beth tried to talk every few days; if they were too busy during the week, however, they made a point to telephone late Sunday afternoon.

"No, Emma invited us to have dinner at her place. And since we were going to be in town later than usual, I thought I'd see if you'd like to come back to the ranch with us for a while. You should have time to finish helping your mother with everything."

"Oh, Beth, I'd love to, but—"

"Jeb said he'd bring you home in time to help with supper. You haven't been out in a long time, and I wanted to show you some of the things we've done to the house—"

"Who is it, dear?" her mother asked then.

"Excuse me a minute, Beth. Mama is talking to me," Darcie said into the mouthpiece and turned to answer her mother. "It's Beth. She and Jeb and the children are in town and want me to go back out to the ranch with—"

"Oh, how nice. You could use a break. You go right ahead, dear. I can manage here."

"Oh, I'll finish helping with dinner and be back in time to help with supper, Mother. But—"

Her mother surprised her by taking the earpiece out of her hand and nudging her away from the telephone. "Beth, what time are you going back to the ranch?"

She listened and nodded at whatever Beth was saying. "She'll be ready in an hour. I'll see to it. And thank you, dear. I think spending an afternoon with you and your family is just what she needs."

Darcie watched as her mother hung the earpiece back onto the telephone. It seemed the matter had been taken out of her hands. How nice it would be to go out to the ranch for the afternoon—rather than having to spend it trying not to run into or away from John Harper.

She and her mother finished setting the dinner dishes on the table and called in the boarders.

"Good timing, Mrs. Malone," Mr. Mitchell said. "That ice cream is frozen hard as a rock. By the time we finish eating, it should be just about right."

Darcie paid little attention to the dinner conversation. Her mind was on finishing the meal in time to freshen up before going out to the Winslow ranch. What a luxury to go. Normally she helped around the house in any way she could on the weekends, and she felt bad about leaving, even though her mother was always trying to persuade her to get out more. It didn't feel right to leave her. She glanced down the table, and her mother smiled at her, reassuring her she was happy her daughter was going out, so Darcie decided to feel good about it, too.

She passed on the ice cream so she could wash the major portion of the dishes before leaving. As she hurried up the back stairs, she heard her mother telling the boarders she was taking a much-needed break for the afternoon.

A few minutes later, she came back downstairs to tell her mother good-bye and go out onto the front porch to wait for the Winslows. She was surprised to find Miss Olivia helping with the dishes and Mrs. Alma having a second bowl of ice cream at the kitchen table.

"Why, how nice of you ladies to help Mama and keep her company in the kitchen!"

"I've told Molly I don't mind helping out around here. And I mean it. It's the least I can do when she's provided me a home."

"You pay me for room and board, Olivia. It's very nice of

you to help out so Darcie won't feel guilty for spending an afternoon with friends."

"Molly, I've lived in other boardinghouses, but I've never felt I had a home until now. You can't put a price on that. As I said, I'm glad to help anytime," Miss Olivia said, drying an ice cream dish.

"What she says is true, Molly." Mrs. Alma added her two cents. "Besides, haven't you been telling me how I need to learn to accept help gracefully?"

Darcie's mother quirked an eyebrow in Mrs. Alma's direction before laughing. "Yes, I have. Guess I need to learn that same lesson, Alma. And, Olivia, thank you for helping me."

"Yes, thank you!" Darcie added. "I feel much better about going off for a few hours now."

"You are both welcome. Actually I think I should be thanking you. It makes me feel part of the family."

Darcie's mother laughed. "Well, I guess we'll have to see what more we can find for you to do around here. I sure like to have my boarders feel at home."

The women's laughter warmed Darcie's heart, and she felt easier about leaving. But then she looked out back and saw John putting the clean ice-cream freezer together and the other men setting out wickets for a game of croquet in the yard. She almost wished she were staying home. Almost.

seven

Darcie fully enjoyed her afternoon at Beth and Jeb's. It was a beautiful April day, warm enough and sunny, without a cloud in the sky. Cassie and Lucas, Jeb's niece and nephew whom he and Beth were raising, couldn't wait to show her the new litter of kittens out in the barn. And they were adorable. Playful calicos, they were hard to resist picking up and cuddling.

Next they visited the apple orchard that would soon be bursting with blooms and the new garden the children had helped Beth plant. They came up with so many things for Darcie to see and do until Jeb decided to take Cassie and Lucas to play with Cal and Liddy McAllister's four children, Grace, Amy, Matthew, and Marcus, at their nearby farm. That way Darcie and Beth could have a good visit by themselves.

Beth made them a pot of tea and brought out some cookies. Her kitchen was light, bright, and cozy, and she had a range that was big enough for the nicest of restaurants. Darcie's mother would have loved it, and she figured that even Emma would be envious of its size. When she commented on it, Beth giggled.

"It is much larger than it looked in the Sears and Roebuck catalogue. Cal and Matt installed it while Jeb's arm was broken. They said they nearly didn't get it in here. Emma has ordered one like it for the café. I'm sure she's going to like it as much as I do!"

Beth fairly glowed as she poured their tea. Marriage certainly seemed to agree with her. "I've never seen you this blissful, Beth. I'm so glad you accepted Jeb's proposal."

"Thank you. I've never been happier. But I didn't ask you to come out here to talk about me. I thought maybe you needed to get out of the house for a while—with John Harper there and all."

"Thank you, Beth. I think it's just what I needed."

"How are things going at home—with him being around all the time?"

Darcie knew Beth was truly concerned for her so she answered honestly. "It's—a little strained, but not quite as bad as I thought it might be. He's very considerate of Mama, and that helps somewhat."

"And makes it tougher in other ways?" Beth asked.

Her friend always had been able to figure out when Darcie wasn't telling everything. But she wasn't ready to get into how confused she was about the contradicting feelings she had for John Harper—at least not now. So all she said was, "Somewhat."

She was thankful when Beth didn't press her anymore and changed the subject. "Well, I'm glad you came out this afternoon. I've wanted you to see what we've done to the house since your last visit. Come on upstairs, and I'll show you the changes we've made there."

As they walked through the dining room and then the parlor on their way upstairs, Darcie was impressed with how beautiful the house had become with their hard work. When Jeb Winslow came to Roswell to raise his deceased brother's children, the house was in an awful state of disrepair. But he'd done a wonderful job of refurbishing it and making it into a showplace. Beth had added her homey touches, and now it was warm and welcoming.

"You know Jeb had finished the major work when we got

married, but since he left most of the decorating to me, I let the children pick out the wallpaper for their rooms. We went through so many sample books that I thought they would never decide on anything." Beth led Darcie upstairs to the bedroom at the end of the hall. "But Jeb and I are pleased with their choices."

Darcie had to agree. For her room, Cassie had chosen a white background with pink roses climbing up green vines. A white coverlet and pink curtains at the windows complemented the paper.

In the room across the hall, Lucas had decided on blue and cream stripes, with a blue comforter and cream curtains.

"They have very good taste, Beth. Their rooms are lovely."

"I agree—I would have chosen the exact same papers for them." She motioned for Darcie to join her in the hall. "Come and see our room."

Darcie followed her down the hall to a larger room at the other end. It was papered in a burgundy and cream stripe, and Beth had made draperies out of burgundy and trimmed them in cream fringe. They were tied back with cream tassels.

The bedroom suite was of oak—all matching pieces. Darcie thought she recognized it as one of the newer styles from the Sears and Roebuck catalogue.

"Oh, this is very nice, Beth," she said. "And your matching dressing table is beautiful."

"Jeb ordered that for me for my birthday. It was too extravagant, but I do enjoy it so!"

Darcie tried not to feel envious, but the sudden longing she felt for a home and family of her own—a husband who cared that much for her—made it hard. And seeing the next room only made it worse.

The small room adjacent to Beth and Jeb's sparkled in

sunny yellow. Beth's sewing machine occupied one corner, and across the room stood a beautiful crib. White curtains hung at the windows, and a white and yellow patchwork quilt covered the feather mattress in the bed.

"Beth?" Darcie whirled to see a grin on her friend's face. "Are you expecting?"

Her friend's joyful laughter and nod answered her question, and Darcie couldn't help but be thrilled for her. "Oh, Beth, that is wonderful! When are you—?"

"In the fall. September, Doc says. Jeb and the children are so excited. And he takes such good care of me."

Darcie sighed. She'd love to be even half as happy one day as Beth looked, with an adoring husband and a baby on the way. Thoughts of a tall young man with brown hair and brown eyes crossed her mind, and he looked a lot like John Harper— Darcie jerked herself out of her reverie. What was she thinking?

She tried to concentrate on Beth's joy as she hugged her. "I am so happy for you! Let's go have another cup of tea and some cookies to celebrate your news!" She had to get out of this room and away from the longing for a home and family of her own. Her life was laid out for her at the moment, and the only man who came to mind was the last man she had any business thinking about.

~

The afternoon had passed pleasantly enough, but John kept watching for Darcie to return while trying not to be obvious about it. It was near suppertime, and the other women were in the kitchen helping Mrs. Malone put together the meal when she came back.

He'd just picked up the Sunday paper from the front parlor and was going to sit on the front porch and read it until Mrs.

Malone called them to the table. Even though he'd been waiting for Darcie, he was taken aback at the sudden leap his heart took at the sight of her coming up the porch steps.

It was getting harder to dismiss the effect she had on him, and he wasn't sure what to do about it. For the moment, he chose to ignore it.

He opened the screen door. "Good evening, Miss Darcie."

"Good evening." She entered the foyer and seemed a little surprised he was opening the door for her.

"I trust you had a good afternoon." He hoped she wouldn't brush by him.

His unspoken prayer was answered as she paused and turned toward him. "It was a lovely afternoon. How was the croquet game?"

John chuckled. "Your mother beat the lot of us."

"She did?" Darcie chuckled and clasped her hands together.

"Twice. But she was very gracious at it."

Darcie smiled, and John wondered if she had any idea how beautiful she was. Somehow he didn't think so.

"Mama is the most gracious woman I know. I'm so glad she had a nice afternoon, too. I'd better go see if I can help her."

John watched her head for the kitchen and was bemused when she turned back. "Thank you for helping Mama have a pleasant afternoon, too."

"I—you're welcome." Surprised by her comment and that they'd almost carried on a conversation away from the dinner table, John wasn't sure what to say next. But Darcie disappeared into the dining room before he could think of a way to keep her talking.

Could she be changing? No. He'd better not read anything into her good manners. A few kind words from her did not mean she'd changed her initial opinion of him, and he'd do well to remember that fact. He found reason to remind himself of that thought several times in the next hour.

Mrs. Malone called everyone in for a supper of thick sandwiches made from the ham left over from their noon meal. They'd finished off the ice cream that afternoon, but she brought out some cookies she'd made the day before.

Everyone wanted to know how Darcie spent her afternoon, so she entertained them with stories of kittens, the orchard, and the changes Beth and Jeb had made to the house. Then she seemed to get a wistful look in her eyes.

"Beth is expecting a baby in the fall."

"Oh, how marvelous!" Miss Olivia exclaimed.

"Doesn't surprise me," Mrs. Alma added.

Mrs. Malone smiled from her place at the other end of the table. "I am so happy for the Winslows. And how nice that Emma's baby will have someone to play with, too."

Darcie nodded but didn't comment.

"It's 'bout time you found someone and married and had a family yourself, Darcie," Mrs. Alma said.

John heard Darcie's quick intake of breath before she answered the older woman.

"Mrs. Alma, I don't have time to find anyone right now. And besides—"

"Why, that's nonsense. You have plenty of opportunity right here—"

"Alma," Mrs. Malone interrupted. "I'm sure when the time is right, Darcie won't have to find anyone. He'll find her."

That seemed to satisfy Mrs. Burton. Or seeing the delicate shade of rose Darcie's cheeks had turned made her realize she might have caused the young woman discomfort with her remarks. "Of course he will," she quickly agreed, then popped a cookie in her mouth and nodded as if to reinforce her words.

"Wonder what the baby will be," Miss Olivia mused out loud.

"It won't matter once it gets here. Whatever it is—boy or girl—it will be exactly what they wanted, I expect," Mrs. Malone said. "I wish I'd had more children. I fear Darcie is too concerned about my welfare—"

"Mama, that is not the case. How could I be too concerned when you were left a widow and we lost near everything Papa worked so hard for—" Darcie clamped her mouth shut and sent a glance in John's direction that chilled him clear through.

There it was again—that thing in the past that caused her to dislike someone with Harper for a last name. He sighed inwardly. He had to find out what it was.

Darcie pushed back her chair and stood. "Would any of you like another cup of coffee?"

"No, thank you, I've had my limit." Mr. Carlton shook his head.

"None for me, either," Mr. Mitchell added.

The ladies shook their heads.

"I'll start cleaning the kitchen then, if you'll excuse me?"

"Of course," Mr. Carlton and Mr. Mitchell said at once.

"I'll be glad to help you," Miss Olivia said.

Darcie smiled at the other woman. "No, thank you. You helped in my absence. Thank you—and you, too, Mrs. Alma—for taking my place this afternoon."

With that, she grabbed several empty plates along with her own and hurried to the kitchen.

Earlier in the foyer, for a moment, John had let himself hope Darcie's opinion of him was changing or at least beginning to.

But after the look she just shot him, he had a sinking feeling that if it had, it wasn't for the better.

❧

Darcie couldn't get to the kitchen fast enough. All that talk at the table of her finding someone and starting a family of her own—when that's what she'd thought about all afternoon. Then to realize the only someone who came to mind was John Harper!

She plunged her hands into the dishwater and began to wash in earnest, shaking her head at the very thought. Well, she wouldn't let her heart go in that direction. Couldn't—

"Darcie, dear. I'm sorry. I didn't mean to upset you," her mother said upon entering the kitchen. "I shouldn't have voiced my thoughts out loud. Please forgive me for making you feel uncomfortable."

"It's all right, Mama. I know you didn't mean to. And I'm sorry if I embarrassed you again. But you must know I'm not looking for anyone. My life—our lives—are too busy to concern myself with—"

Her mother put her hands on Darcie's shoulders and turned her around. "We need to talk, dear." She took the dishrag from her hands and gave her a towel to dry them. "Come and sit down for a minute, Darcie."

From past experience Darcie knew when her mother said, "We need to talk," she meant just that, and she wouldn't let the subject rest until they did. She took a seat at the kitchen table.

Her mother poured them both a cup of coffee. It wouldn't matter if they didn't drink it; it was her custom to talk over a coffee cup. Darcie waited and watched while her mother added a dollop of cream and a teaspoon of sugar to each cup, a sure sign she was concerned or upset. She took her coffee black.

"Mama, you—"

"Please let me speak, Darcie. This has been bothering me for some time now, and I haven't been sure how to broach the subject with you. But tonight you've given me the perfect opportunity."

"But—"

"Darcie." Her mother's raised eyebrow told her to clamp her mouth shut for the moment. She sighed deeply before continuing. "Darcie, you are a wonderful daughter. I couldn't ask for a better one. But I do not expect you to put your life on hold for me. I never have. And it would break your papa's heart to know you are doing that."

She picked up her cup as if to take a drink but only held it with both hands, looking over the rim at Darcie as she kept talking. "You deserve to have the kind of life your friends have. A home and a family of your own to love. I want that for you. Your papa wanted that for you."

"But, Mama, I—"

"I'm not through." Her eyebrow arched again, and she returned her cup to her saucer without taking a sip. "What happened to your papa was awful. Not a day goes by that I don't miss him. I know you do, too. But he would want us to get on with our lives, and he'd be proud of how we've done it, Darcie. We count on the Lord to guide us through each day and aren't beholden to anyone but Him for our living."

Darcie briefly acknowledged she wasn't as good at leaving things in the Lord's hands as her mother was. She needed to do better.

"We can't undo the past," her mother continued. "We can only make the best of our future with the Lord's help. And I want your future to include time with your friends without worrying about me—and a family of your own. And I'd like my future to include grandchildren."

Tears sprang to Darcie's eyes. She wanted those same things. But just wanting them wouldn't bring them about.

"Mama, I know you want that for me, but there is no one—"

"Maybe not right now. But there will be. And when that time comes, I don't want you running away from it because you think you must take care of me. Promise me you won't do that, Darcie."

As any chance of that happening seemed remote, Darcie felt safe in answering her mother. "I promise."

Her mother sighed and leaned back in her chair. "Good. Because the best way you could take care of me would be to provide me with a son-in-law and a passel of grandchildren to love. Maybe one or two who look like your papa."

"Mama. What am I going to do with you!" Darcie could feel the heat steal up her face. She wanted those very same things—more with each passing year. But that was in the Lord's hands.

"You're going to take my advice to heart and quit feeling so responsible for me." As if that was her final word on the subject, her mother finally took a drink of coffee.

Darcie tried not to giggle at the look on her mother's face. But when she stared into her cup, as if trying to figure out how the sugar and cream got there, Darcie could no longer keep from laughing.

"You could have told me," her mother said.

Darcie raised her eyebrow. "I believe I tried to."

Her mother opened her mouth and closed it, then opened it again. "Oh. I guess you did."

She laughed, and Darcie joined her. Shortly their shared laughter filled the kitchen. Darcie was thankful it dissolved some of the earlier tension and ended a very touchy conversation—at least for that night.

eight

Darcie spent the next few days trying to ignore her growing interest in John Harper. But it wasn't easy to do. Ever since the Sunday night he'd greeted her at the door when she came home from the Winslows', her heart went into skittish little spasms each time she saw him.

She didn't know if it was because he was the one person who came to mind when she let herself think of a romantic future. Or if it was the dinner conversation that night when she'd looked at him and realized he'd been in her thoughts off and on all day. And he had rarely been out of them since.

Being at work didn't help, either. Word was getting around it was indeed Douglas Harper's nephew who was seen going in and out of his uncle's old bank. And he was staying at Malone's Boardinghouse.

If Darcie was asked one question a day, it seemed she was asked at least twenty.

From Doc Bradshaw's wife, Myrtle, "Wonder what he's doing here. Do you know, Darcie?"

"He says he's here to settle his uncle's estate, Mrs. Doc. All I know is he works over at the bank most of the day."

"Well, I sure hope he's not going to cause problems for folks around here."

"So do I."

From Nelda Harrison later that afternoon, "Why is he staying at your mother's boardinghouse of all places, Darcie?"

"I don't know why he picked it, Mrs. Harrison." *And I wish he never had.*

"Isn't it a little uncomfortable to have him there?"

That was an understatement if Darcie ever heard one. "A little."

"Well, dear, what in the world was your mother thinking when she rented a room to him?"

Loyalty to her mother had Darcie taking up for her. "She didn't know who he was. Lots of people have that last name, Mrs. Harrison. They aren't all related to Douglas Harper."

"Of course not. I'm sorry, dear. I know your mother couldn't have known who he was when she let him have a room."

And on and on it went, from first one and then another person.

Beatrice Ferguson asked, "Is he going to reopen the bank?"

"I don't have any idea, Mrs. Ferguson."

"Will he be trying to collect outstanding loans?" Iris McDonald wondered.

"I don't know, Mrs. McDonald." Darcie shook her head. She wished she did know. While she prayed she was wrong, that was exactly what she was afraid he might do.

The next day it would start over again, different people, same questions. The questions everyone raised served to keep her own doubts about him foremost in her thoughts. They reminded her this man she'd been dreaming about at night was Douglas Harper's nephew. And that was one fact she couldn't ignore. One she was determined not to let herself forget—no matter how much she might want to.

By Friday she was sick and tired of answering questions while trying not to voice her opinion about John Harper. When Emma called later in the day, it was as if she could tell Darcie was on edge.

"Darcie, are you having a rough day?"

"It'd be better if everyone in Roswell didn't keep asking questions about John Harper. Word has gotten out that he's here, and a lot of people are holding their breath, waiting to see what he's going to do. They seem to think I should know everything, and then I have to go home and—"

"Put up with him there. I'm so sorry."

"No, I'm sorry. I shouldn't be whining about it. Who can I connect you to, Em?"

"I'd like to talk to Liddy, but I'd like to see you, too. Why don't you stop by for some tea on your way home?"

Darcie hesitated only a minute. Her mother had made it plain she wanted her to have a life and spend time with her friends. And besides, she'd be home in plenty of time to help with dinner. "That sounds wonderful, Em—just what I need. I'll be there right after four."

"Good. See you then!"

Darcie connected Emma's line plit to the McAllisters' and sent up a quick prayer of thankfulness for her friends. After telephoning her mother to let her know she'd be a little late, she found herself looking forward to having that cup of tea with Emma.

❧

John felt only frustration. He could find nothing pertaining to the Malones in his uncle's papers. Of course he wasn't halfway finished looking through the files. It could take days, weeks, or even longer to go through them.

Elmer was a great help; but he'd only represented his uncle at his trial, and that was because he'd had to. Then he had become trustee of Douglas Harper's money and written the will leaving everything to John. Other than that, Elmer knew no more than John did about his uncle's business dealings—

except that he'd treated a lot of the citizens of Roswell and the surrounding area badly, and that was common knowledge.

But finding actual evidence of that was not easy. Douglas Harper had his own system for keeping track of his affairs, and it was more than a little confusing to the two men trying to figure it out. John had found records of several foreclosures that seemed legitimate. Then he ran across an entry that included a note not to extend credit anymore, but it seemed the person had been making all their payments on time. Trying to decipher his uncle's bookkeeping system, along with his handwriting, was proving to be a challenge.

By the time he'd put in a full day at the bank, he was ready to leave and go back to the boardinghouse. But, as the week progressed, being at the boardinghouse left him no less exasperated. Darcie was apparently going out of her way to steer clear of him except at the dinner table, and then she seemed to avoid talking directly to him. Yet she listened when he talked to the others. And every once in a while, he found her gaze on him. But the moment she realized he'd caught her looking his way, she would glance away, a delicate pink drifting up her cheeks.

He thought back to the first night before she found out he was related to Douglas Harper. He'd felt then that she'd been as interested in him as he had been in her. But connecting him to his uncle had put an end to any attraction she might have felt toward him. John wished it had done the same for his interest in her.

Instead it seemed to grow with each passing day. The way she came in from work and immediately began helping her mother, her tender concern for Mrs. Burton, and her consideration for her mother's boarders—even though he was sure she didn't like her home being let out to strangers—all of that made his opinion of her rise continuously.

She was even civil to him despite the fact he knew she wished he would find accommodations elsewhere. And perhaps he should. But he couldn't bring himself to look for another place to stay. He didn't want to.

He was probably as comfortable here as he would be anywhere in this town. Most likely more so. For the most part, the other boarders seemed to have accepted him—probably because of Mrs. Malone's example to them. And he'd learned the two gentlemen had not lived in the area when his uncle had been conducting business here, so they didn't seem to have a built-in resentment toward a relation of Douglas Harper. Still, they'd heard rumors, he was sure, and they were loyal to the Malones. One wrong move on his part, and Mitchell and Carlton would have no qualms about seeing him to the door. But as long as Molly Malone let him reside in her home, that was where he would stay.

And no telling how long that will be, no more progress than we've made, John thought, as he sat at his uncle's desk in the bank. He expelled a deep breath and pulled another pile of papers toward him.

&

Darcie was pleased to find that both Liddy and Beth had come into town to have tea with her and Emma again. They went up to Emma and Matt's apartment above the café, where the children could play and the customers wouldn't be disturbed. She was the first topic of conversation.

"You sounded so tired this afternoon, Darcie. Are you all right?" Emma asked.

She sighed and smiled at her dear friends. "I'm fine. It's just that I've been answering questions about John Harper all week. The whole town seems to know he's here, and they—"

"It doesn't take long for that kind of news to spread," Liddy said. "Why, I've even mentioned it to one or two people."

"So have I," Emma said. "Douglas Harper caused enough trouble in this town. If there is to be any more, they need to be warned."

Honest with herself, Darcie realized she probably had a bigger part than anyone in getting the word out. She'd mentioned it to several people the week before, and Jessica had mentioned it to even more. That was all it took to get the news spreading, especially with the telephone growing in use each day.

"And they all want to know why he's here, I'm sure," Liddy said.

"Well, he's only saying he's here to settle his uncle's estate." For a moment Darcie wondered if she'd have found out more if she hadn't thrown such a fit that first night.

"It would be nice if we knew what that meant," Emma said.

With no answers available, the other women nodded in agreement.

"Well, how are things going at home, Darcie?" Liddy asked.

"He's very considerate of Mama," she answered truthfully. Actually he was thoughtful of everyone, even her. No matter how cool she was to him or how hard she tried to ignore him, he was always pleasant to her.

Beth came to her aid. "It's still stressful for you having him there, isn't it?"

In more ways than one. Her confused feelings about the man were wearing her out. "Oh, yes, it is. I think I'll be glad when he settles things and is on his way home."

But once the words were out of her mouth, she realized

they might not be true. More confusion. She sighed deeply and took a drink of tea.

Beth patted her hand while Liddy and Emma nodded.

Feeling the need to change the subject, Darcie prodded Beth to tell the others her news. Liddy and Emma jumped up to hug and congratulate the new mother-to-be, and the next few minutes were taken up discussing babies and growing families.

"At least you have a home large enough for your growing family," Emma said to Beth. "I don't know what Matt and I are going to do. We definitely need a bigger place."

"What will you do with the apartment?" Liddy asked.

"Well, as you might have noticed, Ben has taken on more and more of the management of the café. He's been my helper since I first opened the café, and Matt and I feel his loyalty deserves to be rewarded. We're going to offer it to him if we ever find a place." Emma sighed and shook her head.

"Mrs. Alma's place would be perfect for you if she'd sell it," Darcie said.

"Oh, that's right. She's staying at the boardinghouse, isn't she?" Beth asked.

"Until she recuperates from the influenza. We've been hoping she might decide to stay with us permanently. Her house is much too big for her to take care of now. But—"

"She does love that place. I don't know if she'd ever be willing to sell it." Emma shook her head and looked wistful. "But it would be perfect. I've always loved that place, and it's only a couple of blocks from here."

"Perhaps I can try to see how she'd feel about selling. We haven't actually broached the subject of her staying with us yet." It might well be the answer to keeping Mrs. Alma at the boardinghouse so they could look after her without her knowing that's what they were doing. She was such an independent woman that they didn't dare let her think she couldn't take care of herself.

"Maybe she would be willing to rent to us at first?" Emma asked, smiling.

"That's a wonderful idea, Emma," Liddy said. "That way she'd feel as if she was helping you and Matt while at the same time Darcie and her mother would be helping her."

"And maybe she'd decide to sell to you, Em," Beth added.

"I'll discuss it with Mama tonight and see what we can come up with."

They were all excited, Darcie most of all. Not only did it seem the perfect solution to two of her dear friends' problems, but it also gave her something else to think about besides John Harper.

&

By the time five o'clock rolled around, John was more than ready to leave his uncle's office and the papers piled high on the desk. He'd found nothing that gave him any insight into what his uncle might have done to the Malones. And Elmer Griffin didn't know.

"Let's call it a day, Elmer. I'll buy you a cup of coffee before we head home."

"I'll take you up on that offer. We sure haven't gotten anywhere today, have we?"

"No, we haven't. I think we need more help. Do you know any of the people who worked for Harper Bank who might be willing to help us out?"

"I'm not sure if your uncle's secretary still lives in the area. If we can find her, I'm sure she'd be able to help us; but it's doubtful any of the tellers could enlighten us very much."

John locked up, and the two men took off down the street

toward Emma's Café. He let out a deep breath and shook his head. "I'm not sure anyone but you would be willing to help, even if they could. In case you haven't noticed, I'm not the most popular man in town."

"Don't lose heart, son." Elmer clapped him on the shoulder. "I'll see what I can find out."

"I'd appreciate it, Elmer." At least he seemed to have made one good friend here. John sent up a silent prayer of thankfulness.

He opened the door to Emma's Café as Darcie came hurrying out of it. "Miss Darcie! I wasn't expecting to see you here. Good afternoon."

He must have caught her off guard because her smile didn't suddenly disappear and she appeared to be in a very good mood.

"Nor was I expecting you, Mr. Harper. I'm on my way home to help Mama prepare dinner. Good afternoon to you"—she glanced over at Elmer—"and to you, too, Mr. Griffin."

"Thank you, Miss Malone." He looked from John to Darcie and back again.

Suddenly John knew what he needed to do. He had to talk to Darcie and her mother and find out what his uncle had done to their family.

"Miss Darcie, may I have a word with you before you leave?"

She hesitated for a moment before the manners her mother had taught her prodded her to say, "Of course."

Elmer cleared his throat. "John, I'll go on in and get us a table and order some coffee."

"Thank you, Elmer. I'll be there shortly."

Darcie watched as the older man entered the café, then

turned back to John. "What is it, Mr. Harper?"

He felt he must hurry or Darcie might change her mind. "I wonder if you would ask your mother if I might talk with the two of you after dinner tonight."

"I'll ask her, but knowing my mother, I can assure you she'll agree."

"Good. I—thank you."

"You're welcome. I'd better get going now."

"Yes. Well, I'll see you in a little while then."

She nodded before turning away. "See you at dinner."

❧

Darcie couldn't help but wonder what John wanted to talk to them about. But it didn't matter; she knew her mother would fulfill his request. Darcie didn't think she would refuse to talk to anyone who wished to discuss something with her.

When she arrived home and hurried to the kitchen, she felt a little guilty for taking time for herself, but her mother eased that away by greeting her with a smile.

"I'm glad you had tea with your friends, dear. You should do that more often."

"And what about you, Mama? How often do you get out?"

"Why, Darcie, dear, I get out and about. You're in the telephone office all day. I have the freedom to come and go as I please."

Darcie put on an apron and looked over her shoulder at her mother. "You may have the freedom, but that doesn't mean you use it."

"How was everyone?" Her mother changed the subject deftly. "How are Emma and Beth feeling?"

"They're fine." Darcie began stirring up some biscuits. "Emma is a little worried about the size of their apartment. She and Matt would like to find a larger place."

"Oh, I guess it is about time they found a house."

"You know—Mrs. Alma's place would be perfect."

Her mother stopped stirring the gravy she was making to go with the chicken she'd fried and looked at her daughter. "It would be. It's just the place to raise a family."

"We aren't sure Mrs. Alma would ever agree to sell, though."

"Maybe not right away. But if she thinks someone would love it the way she does—"

"That's what I thought. Maybe she'd agree to rent it to them at first." Darcie cut out the biscuits and dropped them on a pan.

"We'll have to see what we can do about it. I'll try to bring up the subject soon."

The two women grinned at one another as Darcie crossed the room and slid the pan of biscuits in the oven.

"Oh, I almost forgot. I ran into John Harper just outside Emma's. He wants to talk to the two of us after dinner. He wanted me to ask you if it would be all right."

"And you told him?"

"That I was sure you would agree."

Her mother nodded, and Darcie knew she was satisfied. "I wonder what he wants to talk about."

"Yes, so do I."

"Well, we must hear him out, whatever it is. He may have discovered what his uncle did to your papa, or it may be something entirely different."

"And if he has?"

"We'll listen to what he has to say. Darcie, John Harper is a nice young man. I'm convinced he isn't anything like Douglas Harper, and I won't blame him for his uncle's sins. I pray you won't, either."

nine

"Oh, you're back, Darcie." Alma Burton peeked into the room then, saving Darcie from answering her mother. Her gray hair pulled up in a bun and her cheeks taking on more color, she seemed to have a little more energy than when she first came to stay with them. "I was coming to see if I could give your mother a hand with dinner."

Mrs. Alma looked disappointed that Darcie had returned and she wouldn't be needed, but Darcie and her mother assured her they wanted her in the kitchen.

"We can always use an extra hand, Mrs. Alma." Darcie waved her into the room.

"And even if we didn't need help, we're glad to have your company. So come in and stir this gravy while Darcie and I dish up everything. You might taste it and tell me if it needs more salt or pepper, too."

"Well, I ought to be able to manage that. I've made a lot of gravy in my day. I used to love to cook, but it ain't much fun to cook for one."

"No, I don't imagine it is," Darcie's mother said, exchanging a glance with Darcie as Mrs. Alma took the wooden spoon from her and began to stir. "It's also easier to cook for more people, too."

Darcie thought about how lonesome it must be for Mrs. Alma to live alone with no one to care for but herself. For the first time she had a glimpse into why her mother might be happy cooking and caring for boarders and why she insisted she loved what she was doing.

Mrs. Alma sampled a spoonful of the gravy and nodded. "It's real tasty, Molly. But you make great gravy. It's always good and always tastes the same." She laughed. "My brother used to tell me that's what he liked about mine. He said his wife must have 365 recipes for gravy because it tasted different every day."

All three women laughed while they finished setting out the dinner. Darcie was glad her mother had found something for the older woman to do. She seemed to perk up even more from helping that little bit. It would be so good for her to stay here. Darcie wondered if they should broach the subject of selling her house yet, but she would let her mother do it. She had known Alma Burton for a long time and would bring up the subject in the right way and at the right time.

Darcie had almost managed to put the upcoming conversation with John Harper out of her mind, but it only lasted until they met in the dining room. He usually arrived before she did. He had Darcie's chair pulled out for her, but he'd taken to helping Mrs. Alma each night, drawing out her chair and sliding it back to the table for her. If she waited, she was sure he'd help her push her chair closer to the table, too; but there was no need, and she was pleased he saw to the older woman's comfort first. She could tell by the way Mrs. Alma accepted his help without grousing that she liked the young man's attention.

Now as he pulled out his own chair and sat down, Darcie couldn't help but be curious about why he wanted to talk to her and her mother. As the meal progressed from the main course to the buttermilk pie her mother had made, she both dreaded the conversation and almost looked forward to it. It seemed any feelings she had concerning John were consistently—confused.

When the telephone rang their special ring, she exchanged a glance with her mother before hurrying to answer it. It was highly unusual for the telephone to ring during dinnertime, unless she was being called in for work. Tonight proved to be no different.

"Miss Malone?" It was her employer, Mr. McQuillen. "A fire has broken out on South Main, and we need as many volunteers as we can to help fight it. Could you come in to work to help spread the word?"

"I'll be right there, Mr. McQuillen. How bad is it?"

"I can see the flames from here. Try to get here as soon as you can, please." His voice was terse, and Darcie knew it was a true emergency. The town had only one fire wagon.

"I'm on my way." She hung up the earpiece and rushed back into the dining room. "There's a fire downtown. I have to help get out word that they need volunteers."

John stood. "I'll go."

"Yes, so will I." Mr. Carlton wiped his mouth with a napkin.

"As will I." Mr. Mitchell pushed his chair back from the table and stood.

"What is on fire?" Her mother began to clear the table.

"I don't know, Mama. Mr. McQuillen said he could see the flames from the office. I'll let you know as soon as I can, though."

Her mother nodded as Darcie and the three men left the room.

"You men be careful," Miss Olivia called as they rushed out the front door.

In minutes Darcie and the three men were hurrying down the street to the middle of town. They could see the glow before they reached Main Street. Her chest tightened with apprehension. "Oh, dear. I hope it hasn't spread to more buildings!"

The townspeople always feared that. Roswell had grown so much in the last few years that buildings were constructed closer together.

"It's hard to tell from here," Mr. Carlton said.

Once on Main Street, the men dropped Darcie off at the telephone office and started toward the fire. Mr. McQuillen was right. She could see the flames from the office. It was hard to tell what it was—perhaps a hotel or one of the saloons on the south end of town. But it could also be a number of other businesses.

A sense of urgency hit the men, and they suddenly took off running. "Please be careful!" Darcie called out to them. She hurried into the office, praying no one would be injured.

Jessica was already there, along with Jimmie Newland, one of several young men who worked nights, and Mr. McQuillen. He'd divided their customers into four groups and handed Darcie a list of people to contact. She took her place at one of the switchboards and began connecting lines.

As she explained what had happened and asked for volunteers to help with the fire, she tried to fight the thought that kept demanding her attention.

But after Emma called in, she could resist it no longer. "Oh, Darcie, it's you. Good. Matt went down right away, but I haven't had any word since he left. It's been awhile since we've had a fire this size."

"I know. Are you and Mandy and everyone all right? Can you see anything from your apartment?"

"No—only the glow of flames." Darcie could hear her sigh. "I wish I'd get over this, but every time we have a fire of any kind in town, I remember when my place was set on fire. If it hadn't been for Matt—"

"I know, Em. I've been thinking about the same thing. I

hope they can get this put out soon. And I pray it doesn't spread and no one is hurt."

"So do I. Let me know if there's any news, okay?"

"I will. Try not to worry about Matt. I'm sure he'll be fine."

"I'll try. We actually have customers in spite of the fire. I'll keep busy."

Darcie disconnected the line and continued to the next person on her list, but she could no longer avoid thinking about the fire. Talking to Emma had reminded her it was Douglas Harper who hired someone to set Emma's place on fire. She thanked the Lord that Matt had rescued Emma and Mandy and the fire had been put out quickly.

Even though Emma's fire had taken place several years before, it suddenly seemed like only yesterday and brought back memories of Harper's trial and how glad Darcie had been to see him finally put behind bars.

Now they had another fire and another Harper in town. Surely John hadn't had anything to do with this one. Of course not—he'd been right there in the dining room of her own home when word had come about it. Yet his uncle hadn't actually set the fire at Emma's, either. He'd hired someone else to do his dirty work for him. John could have done the same thing.

No. He might be Douglas Harper's nephew, but she couldn't believe he would do something so abominable. Her heart would not let her accept that idea.

❧

The volunteer fire department was hard at work. Two of the men manned the hand pumps on either side of the fire wagon, filling the hose from the water tank, while two more men directed the spray at the burning saloon.

As the fire spread, John was certain it would take the fire

department and the other men who were showing up to get it under control. He was glad he'd come with Mitchell and Carlton. He had the feeling he'd have been run out of town if he hadn't. He wondered why everyone was looking so suspiciously at him, until he remembered Elmer telling him why his uncle had gone to prison. He'd hired someone to set a fire. The very thought that a member of his family could do such a thing sickened him. And yet Douglas Harper had been convicted.

John joined the fire brigade and took his turn filling pails and handing them off to the man in front of him. He couldn't blame the people of this town for the way they felt about Douglas Harper. But he was tired of the fact that the good people of Roswell assumed he was like his uncle. Nothing was further from the truth, but he didn't know how to convince them.

More men showed up, and another line formed in front of a mercantile across the street. At least the artesian wells around Roswell were plentiful. Most businesses had a well and pump on the premises, and tonight they were all being put to good use. Water was drawn from every pump, watering trough, or well within running distance.

As one man threw water on the fire or helped to fill the tanks on the fire wagon, they'd go to the end of the line and the next person would move up. Just as John moved back to the end of the line, two more men showed up to help. They introduced themselves as Cal McAllister and Jeb Winslow and lined up behind John. He recognized them from church and had heard good things about both men at the Malone dinner table.

John filled another pail with water and handed it to Mr. Mitchell. The heat from the flames enveloping the saloon and the café attached to it flared up again. He wasn't worried much about the saloon, figuring the town would be better off with one less. But other businesses could be threatened if the fire wasn't put out soon.

When the second story of the saloon collapsed, burning embers and ashes flew everywhere. The saloon couldn't be saved, so the volunteers concentrated on saving the nearby buildings. It was hours later before the area was considered safe.

Finally John and Mr. Mitchell and Mr. Carlton started back to the boardinghouse. When they reached the telephone office, they looked through the window and saw Darcie still working. John paused. Since the fire was out, she might be leaving soon, and he didn't like the idea of her walking home alone at night.

He glanced at the other two men, who were older and appeared even wearier than he felt. "Why don't you two go on and let Mrs. Malone know that I'll see Darcie home?"

"That's nice of you, Harper," Mr. Carlton said.

Mr. Mitchell wiped his brow with his handkerchief. "Yes, it is. Molly will appreciate it, I'm sure. We'll tell her."

John sat on the bench outside the telephone office and watched the men walk down the street. Mrs. Malone might appreciate his seeing her daughter home, but he wasn't sure Darcie would be of the same mind. He wondered if he should pursue the conversation he'd intended to have with her and her mother. He yawned and shook his head. No. Darcie was probably tired, and he was exhausted. It could wait for another day or two.

ɞ

Darcie stood and stretched. At last the fire was out, and she could go home. She was thankful no one had been hurt and the buildings around the saloon and its café had been saved.

She and Jessica were preparing to leave when Mr. McQuillen came out of his office. "Thank you for coming down, ladies. You've done an important service for the town tonight."

"I hate to think of what might have happened without the telephone in this area," Darcie said. "We could never have gotten out word to enough people in time to help."

"I imagine more than the saloon would have burned to the ground," a male voice said from the doorway.

Darcie's heart did a somersault when she saw John Harper standing there, even though he was covered in soot from fighting the fire.

"I thought I'd see you home, if you have no objection."

In spite of her doubts about his character, her mother was sure he could be trusted. And Darcie was sure she would want her to accept John's offer to walk her home. In truth, she'd had a few qualms about walking home alone at this time of night, too. "I—no—I mean, yes, thank you. That's nice of you. Jessica lives only a street over, so we can see her home, too."

They started down the street with John in the middle of the two women.

"Jessica," Darcie said, "this is John Harper, who is staying at my mother's boardinghouse. Mr. Harper, this is Jessica Landry, my coworker and friend."

Despite the gray ash, John was a very nice-looking man; and from the way Jessica was gazing at him, she didn't seem blind to that fact.

"It's nice to meet you, Mr. Harper. You look very tired. I'm sure it was hard down there fighting that fire."

He did look exhausted, and Darcie was aggravated she hadn't been the one to mention it. But what bothered her most was the stab of jealousy she felt when John smiled at

Jessica and said, "It was pretty warm down there. But it felt good to be of help."

"It does feel good, doesn't it? We were talking about that at the telephone office."

"You both must have worked hard yourselves to round up volunteers. A lot of men showed up."

"Oh, we did." Jessica didn't give Darcie a chance to respond even though John was directing his comments to her. "I'd already contacted quite a few of our customers by the time Darcie got there, but she was such a big help. It took awhile to contact everyone and answer all the questions."

Darcie was glad it was dark because she was sure her jaw dropped an inch or two at Jessica's words. She was certainly trying to make a good impression on John.

"I imagine you were busy," John said.

"Very." Jessica smiled up at him. "But not nearly as busy as you men were."

Darcie wasn't sure what made her jump into the conversation, but she felt a sudden need to do so. "We could have gone home earlier, but by then the switchboard was lit up with people wanting to know what was happening and asking for updates. Mr. McQuillen had gone to his office, and we didn't want to leave Jimmie there to handle it by himself."

By the time they arrived at Jessica's home, Darcie was quite ready to part company with her friend.

"Well, thank you very much for seeing me home, Mr. Harper," Jessica said to John.

"You're welcome, Miss Jessica. It was no problem since it is on our way home."

Darcie's heart warmed at John's words. Jessica looked a little chagrined as she glanced at Darcie.

"Good night, Jessica." Darcie tried to sound pleasant, but

it wasn't easy. She'd never felt so exasperated with the other woman as she was now.

"Yes, well, thank you both. Good night." Jessica ran up the walk to her house. She turned and waved before going inside.

Darcie and John continued down the street. Now that they were alone, she wasn't sure what to say.

"She seems like a nice woman," John commented.

"Mmm," was all Darcie could make herself say. Was he interested in Jessica? She was pretty, and she'd certainly made it clear she was attracted to him!

They walked on in silence as she contemplated why it even mattered to her. Yet it did. But how could she be jealous over a man she couldn't let herself care about and wasn't sure she could even trust?

Darcie had been wondering all evening if John might have had something to do with the fire. And now here he was, his face and hair, his clothes, dusted with ashes from the blaze he'd helped put out. His eyes showed his fatigue. Surely this man couldn't have had anything to do with setting the fire—

"It's been a long evening, hasn't it, Miss Darcie?"

"Yes, it has. I'm so glad no one was hurt in the fire."

John nodded. "It was frightening when the second story fell through. I think we were all afraid the flying embers would catch the nearby buildings on fire, and they almost did. But I'm thankful the Lord took care of that for us."

His faith in the Lord seemed so real and natural that it was becoming increasingly hard not to care about this man. In fact, she was afraid she was already falling in love with him. What was she to do?

ten

The weekend was full of talk about the fire. At the breakfast table on Saturday morning, the ladies wanted a full accounting of what had happened. John left the rehashing of it to Mr. Carlton and Mr. Mitchell. But before putting in time at the bank and going over yet more papers, he decided to inspect the fire damage by daylight. Nothing was left of the saloon and café, but he thanked the Lord the buildings on each side of it still stood. They'd suffered some smoke damage, but that could be taken care of easily enough. It felt good to know he'd helped to save them.

John had hoped that helping with the fire would show the people of Roswell he had their best interests at heart and was not like his uncle. But it didn't take long for him to realize he was wrong.

Returning to the bank, he found some people still shied away from him, crossing the street or ducking into a store. He became more determined than ever to find out why half the town feared him and the other half avoided him.

He'd been at his uncle's desk a half hour when the front door opened. A young couple came inside looking nervous. He quickly stood and walked over to greet them. "Good morning. May I help you with something?"

The young man took off his hat and twisted it in his hands. "My name is Edward Hollingsworth." He touched the shoulder of the woman at his side. "This is my wife, Eileen. I hear tell you're here to settle your uncle's accounts.

We need to talk to you."

"Certainly. Come this way." He led them to the office and motioned them to take a seat. "What can I do for you?"

Edward Hollingsworth cleared his throat. "I—I owed your uncle, and I guess I owe you—now he's gone."

John vaguely remembered the name Hollingsworth in the bank's records. He thought they were among the ones his uncle had charged with too much interest. "You took a loan out with my uncle?"

"Yes. I didn't know who to pay after he went to jail, but now you're here, I guess we need to make arrangements to pay 'fore you decide to take our place away from us."

"Mr. Hollingsworth, I wouldn't do that. I don't even know what you owed my uncle yet. I'm trying to go over his papers, but I don't have a clear picture of anything now. Your account was under your name?"

"Yes, sir. I had to take a loan out several years ago to help pay for some feed and seed. I was late on a payment, and—"

"Your uncle threatened to take the farm." Eileen interrupted her husband. "Edward had to sell one of our work horses to make the payment; then old Harper got arrested before the next payment was due—and we—"

Probably thanked the good Lord for taking him out of business. John could tell she was trying not to cry. He had a feeling this young couple didn't have the money to pay him anything now. He finished the sentence for her. "You didn't know whom to pay. That's perfectly understandable."

The couple glanced at each other, then back at him, as if they couldn't believe his words and were at a loss for what to say next.

"I'm in the process of going over my uncle's papers now." John pointed to the pile of files on the desk. "I'll look up your account and get back to you as soon as I can grasp matters. But don't worry—you'll keep your place."

Edward stood and reached out his hand. "Thank you. We'll pay back what we owe, no matter how long it takes, Mr. Harper."

John shook hands with the man. "I'll be in contact with you once I have a chance to look over your account."

He'd no more than seen them to the door when another man entered with the same kind of story. Jim Benson owed Harper Bank money but didn't know whom to pay after Douglas's imprisonment. He wanted to set up some kind of payment schedule so he wouldn't lose his place. The Benson name sounded familiar also, and John figured he'd seen it among the papers he'd looked at. He'd have to take some of those papers home tonight and go over them again.

"Mr. Benson, I'm in the middle of putting my uncle's papers in order so that I know how to proceed. The only thing I can assure you of this minute is that I have no intention of foreclosing on you."

His words had an immediate effect on the man. John could see relief written on his face as he thanked him and left.

By the time he was ready to call it a day, five different people had paid him a visit, all of them nervous and expecting the worst from him. He tried to assure each of them he was not going to foreclose on their property; but he had the feeling that, much as they wanted to believe him, most were finding it hard to do so.

John felt relieved he could narrow his search for now with names of people who owed his uncle money instead of going painstakingly through the accounts of everyone who'd done business with Harper Bank. But the feeling didn't last long. He hunted for the Hollingsworth and Benson records but didn't see them in the files he was familiar with. What good would it do to have names if he couldn't find the records? He sighed and shook his head. These people had to be accounted for somewhere. First thing Monday morning, he had to see what he could do about getting some help. Maybe Elmer had been able to contact some of his uncle's former employees. He'd pray that at least one or two would agree to help them out.

◆

Not long after the noon meal, Darcie's mother, Miss Olivia, and even Mrs. Alma determined they needed to make the trek downtown to see the damage from the fire. They'd never gone out together for an afternoon so they decided to enjoy tea at Emma's. Darcie's mother rented a surrey so Mrs. Alma wouldn't have to walk, and they headed downtown, along with Darcie.

Looking at it in the daylight, Darcie was even more amazed that nothing else had caught fire. While thankful no one was hurt in the blaze, none of the ladies was the least bit upset a saloon had been destroyed and not some other business. But, as Mrs. Alma pointed out, dampening their mood for the moment, the owner would probably rebuild and be up and running again in a few months.

It was a rare outing for the two Malone women, and Darcie enjoyed the afternoon immensely. Emma's teas had become popular several years earlier. The women of the town had wanted to show their husbands they supported Emma's determination to raise Mandy as her own. She'd made the baby's mother a promise and intended to stand behind it, even though she was unmarried at the time. Most of the men in town, stirred up by Douglas Harper, had fought it; for a while even husbands and wives were at odds. But it was settled to

• everyone's satisfaction when Emma and Matt married.

The women enjoyed the teas whenever they could take an hour or so out of their busy Saturdays. Today Darcie wasn't surprised to see many familiar faces there. Emma had joined their group when Liddy and Beth came in, so they made room at their table and pulled up two more chairs. After inspecting the damage, Liddy and Beth had left their children at Jaffa-Prager Mercantile with their husbands while they came to Emma's for tea.

With Mrs. Alma there, Darcie thought it was the perfect opportunity to bring up Emma and Matt's need for a bigger place to live.

"How are you feeling, Emma?" Darcie's mother asked.

Emma smiled. "Really well—Doc says about three more weeks."

"You're going to be kind of cramped in the apartment, aren't you?" Darcie prompted her.

"Well, yes. I wish we had a larger place to live in, but there's nothing right now. If I'd been thinking correctly, we'd have offered to buy Beth's home when she and Jeb married. But I didn't, and it was snapped up right away. Roswell is growing so fast, nothing is available now. I guess we could build, but. . ." Emma shook her head.

"Would you be willing to rent?" Darcie's mother asked.

"If the right property came available, I'm sure we would. But there's not much available there, either."

"Well, I'm sure something will turn up," Darcie assured her. "We'll all pray about it for you."

"Thank you. I'm confident the Lord will provide something. I just need to learn patience."

Darcie and her mother exchanged a look, and she knew they were both hoping Mrs. Alma would take the conversation to heart. She might not comment now, but she'd no doubt heard every word.

The conversation turned to the fire. Everyone wondered, Was it set or was it an accident?

"Who would do something like that? And why?" Miss Olivia asked.

"A competitor possibly?" Darcie's mother suggested. "Someone who wanted to put the saloon out of business."

Mrs. Alma chuckled. "In that case, Molly, any one of us at this table could be the culprit."

They laughed at the truth in her words.

"Well," Mrs. Alma added, serious now, "at least we don't have to worry about Douglas Harper being behind it this time. He's gone."

Quiet suddenly descended on the table, and Darcie wondered if the others were remembering Douglas Harper had gone to prison for burning Emma's place. Had it not been for quick action by Matt and Ben and the fire department, Emma's Café might not be here now. She also wondered if they were questioning, as she had, whether his nephew might have had something to do with this one. It didn't take long for her to find out.

"Strange that his nephew is here, though, isn't it?" Liddy asked.

Emma nodded. "It does seem a little odd, doesn't it? I have to admit I've wondered if he could have had anything to do with setting this fire. I know it's because he's related to the man who was responsible for setting my café on fire, but still—"

Darcie took a sip of tea. Obviously she wasn't the only one a little suspicious, but somehow that didn't give her any comfort.

"Well, he was at my dinner table last night," her mother said with authority. "There's no way he could have had anything to do with it."

Liddy shook her head. "I don't think that would prove anything, Mrs. Malone. Douglas Harper didn't actually set Emma's Café on fire. He hired someone to do it."

It was very hard not to speculate if the man's nephew could have had anything to do with this one, Darcie thought. And yet hearing her friends voice the same suspicions she had suddenly made her want to take up for John. But what Liddy said was true, and how could they be certain? She wanted so badly to be sure he didn't have anything to do with it.

"That nice young man wouldn't do a thing like that," Mrs. Alma said.

"I agree," Darcie's mother said. "He wouldn't. And we can't judge him on the basis of who he's related to."

"I wouldn't count on everyone agreeing with you two ladies." Emma shook her head. "I've heard a lot of comments from my customers, and most are distrustful of anyone with the last name Harper."

"That's true," Liddy agreed. "But Cal told me he and Jeb worked side by side with John Harper last night and no one worked any harder."

"I know. Matt didn't work alongside him, but he said he saw him trying to put out that fire with as much energy as everyone else there," Emma added.

"It's hard not to remember what his uncle did."

"I've been a pretty good judge of character all my life," Mrs. Alma said. "And I tell you this—Douglas Harper was the worst kind of scoundrel, but his nephew is nothing like him. Quite the opposite, in fact."

Darcie found herself praying Mrs. Alma was right.

❧

That night at supper, John was his usual considerate self, helping Mrs. Alma with her chair and complimenting her mother on the meal; but he was quiet, and his eyes looked sad.

"Are you all right, John?" her mother asked. Obviously Darcie wasn't the only one who seemed to think he wasn't himself.

"I'm fine, Mrs. Malone."

"You didn't breathe in too much of that smoke last night, did you?" Mrs. Alma asked.

"No. Really, I'm fine. I'm sorry if I appear rude tonight. I just have my mind on other things."

Darcie couldn't help but wonder what other things he was thinking about.

"That fire was something, wasn't it?" Mr. Carlton said.

"It certainly was," John said.

"I've never put out a fire before," Mr. Mitchell said. "It was very satisfying to be able to help."

"Made me feel ten years younger to keep up with the likes of John here and the deputy," Mr. Carlton added.

"You both certainly pulled your weight," John said.

The older men had been proud of themselves, and Darcie figured they had a right to be; but their smiles were looking a little smug to her. On the other hand, she wished John would smile, but he seemed miles away. What was he thinking about? The fire? His uncle's business? Jessica? That last thought didn't sit well with her, but then neither did the sudden pang of jealousy she felt.

John still seemed to be deep in thought when he asked, "Mrs. Malone, would you happen to know any of the people who worked at my uncle's bank? I could use some assistance in going over some of his records."

Darcie's mother thought for a moment. "I believe his secretary was a—Charlotte Mead? Does that sound right, Alma?"

Mrs. Alma nodded. "Yes, Charlotte worked for him."

"Does she still live around here?"

"I believe she does. Last I heard, she was living over on Sixth Street."

Suddenly John's mood lightened. "Thank you! I should have thought to ask you ladies that question long ago. I'll try to reach her on Monday if Elmer hasn't already. He was going to try to contact some of the former employees for me. My uncle treated some people in this town badly, and I need help in reading his special way of keeping records."

Darcie and her mother could tell him a few things about Douglas Harper's bad dealings. But he hadn't mentioned the talk he'd wanted to have with them on Friday again, and they still didn't know what he wanted to discuss. And much as Darcie wanted to find out some things herself, she knew her mother wouldn't bring up the subject of how his uncle had treated her family. She would leave it to John to bring it up.

❧

The next morning Darcie's mother insisted they wait for John to accompany them to church, so she found herself lingering in the foyer with her mother and Mrs. Alma. Could he have meant what he said last night? Did he believe his uncle had treated people badly? And what did he intend to do about it if he found out it was true?

John came downstairs and smiled when he saw the three women had waited for him. "What an honor to be escorting three lovely ladies to church this morning!"

His gaze rested on Darcie, and she was glad she'd dressed in one of her favorite outfits, a blue and white linen suit with a big sailor collar. A blue hat with silk flowers and a white plume, along with a blue purse, completed the ensemble, leaving her feeling confident she looked her best.

John appeared to be in a much better mood. Maybe he'd just been exhausted from working the fire on Friday night and needed a good rest. Whatever it was, Darcie was relieved he didn't look as tired as he had the night before.

Once they'd entered the church building, she noticed some of the members glancing at John with a look of fear or even anger on their faces while a few whispered to each other. As they walked up the aisle to the pew she and her mother normally sat in, Darcie found herself feeling uncomfortable for John's sake.

But Minister Turley's sermon, based on Proverbs, chapter twenty-six, verse twenty, pricked her heart and gave her much to consider for the rest of the day: "Where no wood is, there the fire goeth out: so where there is no talebearer, the strife ceaseth."

She'd been so upset about John Harper living in her father's home that she had complained loud and often to those who would listen. But had she also become a talebearer, causing strife for John?

eleven

By the time John arrived at the bank on Monday morning, two or three people had crossed the street to avoid him. He wondered if they'd been in debt to the bank. After Saturday, he knew many were afraid he would foreclose on their property, and it struck him that his uncle must have demanded collateral for a lot of the money he lent. Of course, that in itself wasn't wrong, but from some of the entries he'd seen, it appeared the man had demanded more than the norm.

He hoped Elmer Griffin had contacted some of his uncle Douglas's former employees over the weekend and that they would be willing to help out. If not, he would have to take out an advertisement in the local paper and pray that someone would answer it and apply to help them.

Elmer entered the bank around nine o'clock with someone following him. John was afraid yet another person had come to let him know he owed Douglas Harper money and wanted to find a way to pay it back.

This was a woman of about fifty, neatly dressed in a gray-striped skirt and matching jacket, her silver-gray hair pulled into a bun at the back of her neck. When she hesitated just inside the door, John's heart flared with hope that the older man had found some help.

"John, this is Charlotte Mead, your uncle's former secretary. She's here to help us out if you can convince her you mean no one harm." John crossed the room to where she stood as Elmer continued. "And Miss Mead, this is John

Harper. As I mentioned earlier, he's here to settle his uncle's estate; but he's heard how Douglas treated the people in this area, and he wants to put things right—if he can."

"I know that's what you told me, Elmer. But after Douglas went to prison and I helped people get their money out of the bank, I said I'd never set foot in here again."

"I can understand how you might feel that way, Miss Mead," John said. She had such a sad look in her eyes, bright blue and large behind her glasses, that his heart went out to her. He took one of her hands in his and gazed directly into her eyes. "I need your help. I would like to bring honor back to my family name in this town, but I don't think I can do it without your assistance. I want to set things right."

Miss Mead's gaze met his and held it for several moments before she slowly nodded. "Elmer has assured me you are a good man—I hope he is right. What do you need me to do?"

John let out his breath. "Elmer and I have had an awful time trying to decipher my uncle Douglas's handwriting for one thing. And I'm having difficulty locating complete files on people who are coming to me and saying they owed my uncle money."

"I thought you said you wanted to help. Do you want me to help you foreclose on those people and collect the outstanding debts instead? Because I won't—"

"No, ma'am. I don't want to foreclose on anyone. But I would like to settle the accounts. I need to know what these people are talking about. I can find records on only a few, and I suspect my uncle's business practices left much to be desired. I need your help in sorting it all out. Will you do that for me—for the people of this town, Miss Mead?"

She tilted her head and gave him a long look. "All right," she said. "I'll be back this afternoon, and we can get started then. It's time someone 'sides me knows what Douglas Harper was really like."

❧

Talk of the fire hadn't died down by Monday, and all morning people were ringing in to Roswell Telephone and Manufacturing Company specifically to talk to Darcie about it. Most voiced their opinions that it could have been John Harper.

"I tell you, Darcie—the sheriff needs to look at your mother's boarder—that nephew of Douglas Harper," Nora Hanson had said. "You know, it was setting Emma's place on fire that sent Douglas to prison."

Hearing it expressed like that made Darcie cringe. While she wasn't sure what John was going to do about settling his uncle's business, she'd become almost certain he had nothing to do with the fire.

"I don't think he had anything to do with it, Mrs. Hanson. Why, he was at our dinner table when we found out about the fire. He even helped put it out."

"Humph. That doesn't mean anything. He could have been trying to convince everyone he didn't when he did."

Nora wasn't the only one to voice her suspicions of John. All through the morning, when Darcie tried to take up for him, she was reminded she had been the one to express her distrust of the man when he first arrived in town.

"Darcie," Mrs. Waller said, "I know you are just as suspicious as the rest of us. How can you not be? He's Douglas Harper's nephew after all, and that man was probably the cause of your papa having that stroke. You told me you doubted him only a few weeks ago."

Once more she was reminded why she couldn't trust John Harper. It didn't matter that she was beginning to care way too much for him, whether she wanted to or not. Darcie couldn't deny what Amelia Waller was saying. She had voiced her distrust of the man to as many as would listen to her, especially in those first few days after people found out Douglas Harper's nephew was in town.

By that afternoon, Darcie had to face the fact it was indeed possible she had planted the seeds of suspicion in the minds of her friends and others she'd talked to since John Harper had arrived in town. And she'd even used her place of work to do it—something she'd been determined not to do after she was promoted.

Suddenly she realized that not only had she not been doing her job as she should, but even more important, she hadn't been acting in a Christian way. She had become a talebearer stirring up strife. And if John Harper intended to do the right thing, then she had wronged him horribly by churning up bad feelings. Tears sprang to her eyes as she closed them and said a silent prayer, asking the Lord for His forgiveness and to show her what to do to make things right.

❧

John and Elmer were looking forward to working when Miss Mead returned and decided to have their noon meal at Emma's Café before then. While Emma was civil to John, most of her customers turned a cold shoulder to the two men.

After giving their order, John turned to the older man. "Elmer, I'm sorry that helping me out seems to be ruining your reputation around here."

Elmer shook his head. "Don't worry about it. The fire brought up old memories for a lot of these people. One of these days they'll discover you're nothing like Douglas."

John was beginning to think that would never happen. "Elmer, can you tell me what you know about my uncle's business association with the Malones?"

"No, son, I don't know anything about that. Maybe Miss Mead will."

John hoped so. Because of the fire, he'd had to delay talking with them, but it was time now. He had to find out why Darcie was determined to dislike him from the moment she found out who he was. He'd waited long enough.

❧

When Charlotte Mead came back that afternoon, she was lugging two leather file cases. John and Elmer hurried to help her with them.

"What do we have here, Miss Mead?" Elmer asked.

"These are the records I took home with me when Douglas Harper went to jail. If you remember, I helped the sheriff's office make sure people got their money out of the bank." Miss Mead looked at Elmer. "You remember that, Mr. Griffin?"

Elmer nodded.

"But some owed money to the bank, and I didn't know what to do with those records. I didn't want those people to be hurt any more than they already had been, so I took 'em home with me. I prayed after I went home, and I'm trusting in the Lord and in you, John Harper, to do what is right by these people. It'll take awhile to explain it all to you. As you've already discovered, your uncle had his own bookkeeping system."

By midafternoon John had figured out his uncle's schemes were worse than he'd thought. He'd wanted to own as much of Roswell and the surrounding area as he could—and by any means necessary. And after reading the few records they were able to decipher with Charlotte Mead's help, he understood why anyone who had done business with Douglas Harper once wouldn't want to have anything else to do with another man named Harper.

John finally grasped why the Hollingsworths and Mr. Benson and the others feared he might foreclose on their property; his uncle made it a practice to foreclose after only one or two missed payments. And he had lent money at such high interest rates that it was almost impossible for the normal person to make every payment.

When Miss Mead pulled out the Malone file, John held his breath. His uncle Douglas had planned to foreclose on the family holdings shortly before Darcie's father died.

"What happened after Mr. Malone passed away, Miss Mead? Do you have any records of that?"

She thought for a minute and pulled the second file case toward her. "I believe Mrs. Malone signed over all the holdings except for the house in town and the cash on hand."

"And he let her?"

"Yes, he did. Your uncle—"

"Deserved to go to prison." John slammed shut the ledger he'd been reviewing and stood. He strode to the window and looked out on this town his uncle had planned on owning. It had been so hard for him to comprehend the kind of man his uncle was that at first he'd wanted to give him the benefit of the doubt. Maybe he had been accused wrongly—maybe he'd been misunderstood—maybe—maybe—maybe. Over and over again John had tried to understand a person he'd never even known. Now he knew he would never comprehend the mind of his father's brother. Nor did he want to.

But he did want to grasp the full story of what he'd done, and he knew the bank records alone couldn't tell him. It was time to pay a visit to the sheriff's office—to find out the truth, no matter how painful it might be.

"Let's call it a day," John said. "Miss Mead, I can't thank you enough for your help. You'll be here tomorrow?"

He held his breath for a moment as the older woman studied him, seeming to take his measure, deciding what kind of man she thought he was. Only when she smiled and nodded did he breathe.

"I can see you want to right the wrongs your uncle did, Mr. Harper. I'll be here first thing in the morning."

"I'll see Miss Mead home," Elmer offered.

"Why, thank you, Mr. Griffin," Miss Mead said.

John walked them both to the door and silently thanked the Lord for helping Elmer reach Charlotte Mead—and for her willingness to help. With her assistance, today had been more productive than all the days he and Elmer had put in trying to make sense of his uncle's handwriting. But today's revelations raised even more questions. John locked up and headed toward the sheriff's office. He had to have some answers.

The sheriff wasn't in, but a deputy was. He was pouring a cup of coffee when John entered the office.

"Afternoon, Mr. Harper. I'm Deputy Matt Johnson. What can I do for you?"

John was taken aback the deputy knew who he was. He didn't recall being introduced to him. But then nearly everyone knew who he was by now. Most didn't want to, though.

"I have some questions I'd like answered if you have a minute."

"I do. Want a cup of coffee?"

John shook his head. "No, thank you."

"Well, take a seat." The deputy motioned to the chair facing the desk. "What do you want to know?"

John leaned forward, his elbows on his knees, his hands laced together. He looked at the floor a moment before meeting the deputy's gaze. "I've been reviewing"—he paused, unable to say "my uncle"—"Douglas Harper's records. But they aren't telling me everything. I'm hoping you can tell me more."

"I won't have anything nice to say about him."

"I don't figure anyone in town will."

The deputy nodded. "You're right. A lot of people in this town came to despise the man."

"I realize that, and I'm sure they had good reason. But I'd like to know the facts that don't show up on paper."

"I see. All right. Where do you want me to start?"

"With whatever I need to know to try to undo some of the harm he did to this town."

"You sure you want to know it all?" The deputy leaned back in his chair.

"I have to. My family name is at stake here."

"You know he went to prison for hiring someone to set fire to my wife's café across the street?"

John nodded. "I'd heard that. But what I don't know is why he would do something like that? I mean, what possible reason—?"

"Douglas Harper knew the railroad here would extend all the way to Amarillo. He wanted to own as much of the town as he could. Emma's Café is on prime property, close to everything. But Emma never did business with him. He'd tried to get her to sell out to him several years before, to no avail. So he just decided to run her out of town. First he tried to take Mandy away from her."

"Your child?"

John shook his head. "No. We weren't married then. Mandy's mama was one of Emma's employees. She got sick, and before she died, she asked Em to take Mandy in and raise her as her own if she didn't make it. Of course Em agreed, and when Anna died, she took in Mandy."

"And Douglas wanted the child?"

"No. He just wanted to cause Em problems. He even convinced the town council to give her a deadline for finding a husband so she could keep Mandy. We figured he wanted to make it so hard on her to keep the child that she would sell out and move away." Matt chuckled. "He didn't know Em. She dug her feet in and stayed. She put in an advertisement for a husband, and, well, to make a long story short, I answered. It was at the town meeting where we told them we were married that the truth came out about your uncle. He'd hired someone to set fire to the café, then had another lined up to buy her out if need be so he'd get the property. When he was finally arrested, I think half this town breathed a collective sigh of relief. After all the things he'd done to people around here, finally he was going to pay."

It was so hard to take in. John stood. "I think I'd like that coffee now."

"Help yourself."

John poured a cup of the strong brew and sat back down. "What else can you tell me?"

"Well, let's see. He tried to blackmail Em's best friend, Liddy, into marrying him to pay off the debt her first husband owed after he died. She was expecting at the time. Cal McAllister helped her out by leasing some of her land so she could make payments. Once Cal finally convinced Liddy to marry him, he took great pleasure in paying Harper off for good."

It kept getting worse. John had no doubt that what the deputy was telling him was true, but it was so hard to believe anyone could be so repulsive. He had to ask the next question. "What about the Malone family? Did he have anything to do with Mr. Malone's death?"

Deputy Johnson leaned forward and propped his elbows on his desk. He sighed. "He didn't pull out a gun and shoot him, if that's what you mean. But most of us believe he put enough stress on the man to cause his death. Charles Malone was one of the most respected ranchers around these parts— didn't owe anyone a dime. In fact, most times he was helping others. Was doing real good—even bought the house in town a few years before.

"Then we had a year of drought, and he lost a lot of cattle. 'Bout the time he was pulling out of that, we had a real bad winter, and Charles lost most of his herd in one blizzard. He wanted to build his herd back up, so he went to Harper for a loan to buy more cattle."

"Why would he have gone to him if everyone knew how he did business?" John asked.

"He didn't know at the time. Keep in mind that at first no one had any idea what kind of man Harper was. He could be charming when it suited him, and obviously it suited him well enough to get a seat on the city council. No one knew his motive then was to acquire as much land around here as he could. That came out after Emma's place was set on fire."

So his uncle's claim to the family of being one of the most influential people in town hadn't been a total lie. He only neglected to say what kind of influence he wielded or that he'd also become one of the most hated men in town.

John took a drink of coffee, trying to grasp all that Deputy Johnson was telling him. "From the bank records I've just examined, I know Mr. Malone had trouble making the payments. Of course, at the rate of interest my uncle charged, most people would find it hard to make them."

The deputy nodded. "The winter after Charles took out

the loan was almost as bad as the one before. He lost more cattle and was in trouble. Harper started demanding payment, and, well, I guess the stress of it all took its toll. Charles collapsed in his office at the ranch. Doc said he died of a stroke, but we don't know for sure what caused it. All I know is that the worry Harper put Charles through sure couldn't have helped his health any."

"No. I'm sure it didn't. And Douglas didn't let up on Mrs. Malone, did he?"

"No. And with no real way to pay him, Molly finally signed over the ranch and all other holdings to him. All except for the house in town and enough money to get her boardinghouse started. She did make sure he marked the loan paid in full."

John felt physically sick that a member of his family could have caused people so much pain. It was bad enough that his uncle's business practices with men were so corrupt, but the fact that he seemed to delight in making women miserable was appalling. No wonder no one in this town mourned the death of Douglas Harper.

twelve

When Darcie left work for home on Monday and saw John entering the sheriff's office, she couldn't help but wonder what business he had there. Could he be trying to enlist the sheriff's help in collecting money owed the bank?

No. She shrugged off that thought. From what he'd told them on Saturday evening, he believed his uncle had not treated people right and wanted help in getting to the bottom of things. Maybe he was asking for the sheriff's help in that.

Or it could be— Darcie's heart seemed to stop beating for a moment. Feelings were running high against him in this town. She hoped he hadn't received some kind of threat. She hurried home, trying to put that thought out of her mind, too. If that were the case, she would have to bear the guilt for helping fuel the flame of anger at him.

"Dear Lord, please, I hope and pray John has not been threatened in any way, particularly not because of my words. But if he has, please keep him safe," she whispered as she ran up the front steps of her home. But her heart was heavy because she knew that, even if he hadn't been threatened, she had stoked the fire of resentment toward John Harper.

She rushed upstairs to change clothes and then back down to help her mother in the kitchen, happy to see that Mrs. Alma was there, also. She was stirring up some corn bread to go with the pinto beans simmering away on the back of the stove. Darcie set to work helping her mother peel the potatoes she'd fry to go with them. A simple meal, it was one of the boarders' favorites. She could smell the apple crisp her mother had in the oven for dessert.

"How was your day, dear?" her mother asked.

Enlightening. Much more so than Darcie would have liked. She had to face some distasteful facts about herself. But she didn't say that. "Busy."

"We've been busy here today, too," her mother said. "We had a slight emergency. Olivia fell down the stairs. We thought she broke an ankle. It was right after you left for work. We were thankful Mr. Carlton was still here. He telephoned Doc Bradshaw while Alma and I saw to Olivia."

"Oh, no! Is she all right?"

"Yes, she is. It's only a bad sprain, and nothing was broken. Alma helped me get her settled in the back parlor after Doc said the stairs would be hard on her for a few days." Darcie's mother set a big iron skillet on the range, added some bacon grease to it, and turned on the fire under it. "She's going to have to stay there for the time being. The gentlemen will have to keep to the front parlor until she can make it up and down the stairs again."

"I'm sure they won't mind." Darcie sliced the last potato, then chopped an onion for her mother to add right before the potatoes were finished cooking.

"No, they won't, I'm sure." Her mother took the bowl of potatoes over to the stove and carefully emptied the contents into the skillet. The sizzling sound confirmed that the grease was just right. "I gave her a little bell to let me know when she needed something, and she's—"

"About worn it out already," Mrs. Alma said. "She needed water; she needed her pillow fluffed; she wanted some company.

And all that before the medicine Doc gave her made her drowsy enough to sleep."

Darcie's mother chuckled. "I don't know what I'd have done without Alma today. Olivia would have run me ragged, poor dear."

"I'm going to teach her to knit. I think she needs something to occupy her time."

"See?" Darcie's mother said. "I need Alma here. I've been trying to convince her to stay with us permanently. I so enjoy her company."

Darcie exchanged a glance with her mother before adding her own thoughts on the subject. "Oh, Mrs. Alma, it would be so nice if you stayed on with us."

"And I wouldn't want any rent from you, Alma. Just your company. You are like family."

Alma shook her head, but they could tell she was pleased they wanted to keep her there. "I'm thinking on it."

"You know, I never knew my grandparents that well with their being back East and all." Darcie crossed the room to the sink and pumped water out to wash the onion off her hands. "I've always thought of you sort of like a grandmother. I'd love for you to stay with us."

"I think that's the nicest thing anyone has said to me in a long, long time, Darcie," Mrs. Alma said. "Thank you."

"It's the truth." Darcie turned around and wondered if the sudden sheen she saw in the older woman's eyes was tears.

Just then Mrs. Alma wiped her eyes with the hem of her apron, but she didn't admit to sentimentality being the cause of them. She pushed the bowl of onions across the table. "Them are the hottest onions I've seen in a while. They're 'bout to make me cry."

Darcie and her mother agreed with their friend. Suddenly it seemed they were fighting tears right along with her.

"Those must be mighty strong onions," her mother said, wiping her eyes with the back of her sleeve.

❧

By the time John left the sheriff's office, he felt emotionally drained. The thought that he was related to a man like Douglas Harper repulsed him. It had been hard enough to let his family know the man had died in prison. How would he tell them it was no less than he deserved?

The deputy had told him about others who had suffered from his uncle's greed. Jed Brewster, for one. Douglas had paid Jed to cause a disturbance at Emma's, then tried to blackmail him into scaring Emma by throwing a rock through one of her windows. He refused to do that and was a witness in Douglas's trial. When that hadn't worked, evidently his uncle hired a man called Zeke to throw the rock and later set the fire.

John's head was still reeling from what he'd found out. And while he was sure that what the deputy had told him was true about the Malones, he still felt the need to hear it from them—to hear firsthand how his uncle had impacted their lives. Somehow he had to find a way to bring up painful memories for them. But he wasn't looking forward to it.

He cared about those two women. Mrs. Malone reminded him of his mother, and Darcie—well, she had found a place in his heart whether she wanted to be there or not. After hearing their story from the deputy, though, he knew he would have to accept the fact that she wanted nothing to do with him. He couldn't blame her.

As he hurried up the porch steps to the boardinghouse,

he knew none of that would stop his pulse from racing whenever she came into view. Even now, as he entered the house and heard female laughter issuing from the kitchen, he wished with his whole heart they'd met under different circumstances. He sensed she would be all he could ever want in a woman, and if things had been different—but they weren't. He had to be grateful the Malones hadn't turned him out on his ear.

Instead Mrs. Malone had let him stay when her daughter would have made him go. Even then Darcie had treated him as graciously as she could, for her mother's sake to be sure. Under the same circumstances, John wasn't sure he'd have been as civil.

As he climbed the stairs to his room to freshen up, the smell of dinner had his stomach growling. When he started back down, he thought he heard a faint jingle. And then another. Only when he reached the ground floor did he realize he was hearing a bell. The sound was coming from the back parlor. He watched Darcie and her mother disappear behind closed doors.

Darcie emerged a moment later. "Oh, good, you're home. I was going to the front parlor to look for one of the men. Mr. Harper, would you help us get Miss Olivia to the dining room?"

"Why, of course. Is something wrong with her?"

"Oh, I'm sorry. Of course you don't know. She fell and sprained her ankle badly this morning and for the time being will be staying here in the back parlor. Doc left her some crutches, but Mama thought it might be easier this first day if one of you could carry her into the dining room."

"Oh, certainly. I'll be glad to." John was more than happy to help. And he wished he could keep Darcie talking. This was the most conversation they'd had in a while.

"Thank you. Mother is helping her get presentable." Darcie smiled the way that always made his heart beat a little faster. "We're afraid it might be too painful for her to sit at the table, but she doesn't want to take dinner in here by herself."

"That's understandable."

Just then Mrs. Malone opened the doors. "Oh, good. Darcie found you, John. I believe Olivia is ready. Let me call our other boarders to dinner, and you can bring her in."

John was glad Darcie stayed with him as he entered the back parlor. Miss Olivia looked frail sitting on the settee with her feet propped up.

"Miss Olivia, I'm so sorry about your accident. Let me see if I can get you to the dining room without your suffering too much pain." John lifted her into his arms effortlessly and turned toward the hallway.

Darcie picked up a small footstool to take with them and made sure nothing was in his way before following him as he carried Olivia through the house. The other diners were already seated when he brought her in. John and Darcie helped Miss Olivia get as comfortable as possible amid the questions and concern about her ankle.

John set her gently in her chair, and Darcie scooted the stool under the table so she could prop her foot on it.

"Thank you so very much," Miss Olivia said as John and Darcie took their seats. "You all are so kind to me."

Dinner passed pleasantly enough, with a recounting for everyone about what exactly happened to Miss Olivia. John put talking to the Malones about Douglas Harper on hold again for the time being. Of course he wouldn't bring it up at the dinner table anyway, but he was determined to talk to them tonight. He couldn't delay it any longer.

&

Because the Malones had to help Miss Olivia settle down and had to do the dishes, John had to wait awhile before talking to them, so he went for a walk after dinner.

When he returned an hour later, he found Mr. Carlton and Mr. Mitchell deep in thought over their chess game in the front parlor. In the back parlor, Mrs. Alma was giving knitting instructions to Miss Olivia. He was pretty sure the murmur from the kitchen indicated Darcie and her mother were cleaning up. He might never have a better chance to talk to them than now.

He started whistling before he reached the kitchen so they wouldn't think he was eavesdropping on their conversation. By the time he stood in the open doorway, Mrs. Malone was welcoming him with a smile.

"Why, John, what can I do for you? Would you like a cup of coffee or something cool to drink?"

"No, thank you." He dreaded this, but at the same time he wanted to get it over with. "I—I'd like to talk to you and your daughter if I may."

Mrs. Malone glanced at her daughter. An unspoken question must have passed between them because Darcie gave her mother a slight nod.

"Come right in." Mrs. Malone motioned to him to take a seat at the table. "But I'm going to have a cup of coffee. Are you sure you don't want one, too?"

"Might as well—she'll end up pouring you one anyway," Darcie said, handing her own cup to her mother. "Mama thinks you have to have a cup to hold if you sit at the kitchen table for long."

Mrs. Malone chuckled, pouring the second cup for Darcie. "She's right. I do."

John nodded. "Then, yes, please, I'd like a cup." Maybe having a cup to hold would somehow make this conversation easier.

Mrs. Malone brought him a full cup and placed sugar and cream on the table before she and Darcie joined him there. She took a sip from her own cup, then looked him straight in the eyes. "What did you want to talk about, John?"

He grasped the cup in front of him and stared down into the warm, aromatic liquid. It was time. *Please, Lord, help me do this right and not cause these two women any more pain than they've already suffered from my uncle.*

He looked into Mrs. Malone's eyes. The expression in them was kind and caring, and John suddenly knew she didn't blame him for the pain in her past. It gave him the strength to go on. "I talked to my uncle's secretary today. And then I talked to Deputy Johnson. But I need to hear the truth from you." He paused, taking in a deep gulp of air and letting it out again, before asking the question he most needed answered. "Did my uncle cause your husband's death?"

For a moment it was as if no one breathed. It was so quiet in the kitchen, he could hear the sound of the pendulum swinging on the clock in the foyer and the soft murmur of voices elsewhere in the house. John looked from one woman to another, waiting for an answer he didn't want to hear.

"Yes," Darcie said thickly.

"He put my husband through a lot of stress." Her mother picked up her cup and held it close to her chest. "I believe all the worry became too much for him."

"Can you tell me what happened?"

Mrs. Malone bit her bottom lip, and tears welled up in her eyes.

John wanted to tell her "never mind," but he felt he must find out what he had to make right.

"Mama, you don't have to. I can tell him."

"No." Her mother shook her head. "I will. He needs to know. My husband was a very successful rancher. He started with a small herd and built it to one of the largest in these parts by the time we'd been married ten years. Charles worked hard to get to the point where people came to him for advice or a quick loan, and he never turned down anyone as far as I know. We prospered, and he built the house in town so we'd be closer to church and school and be more a part of the community." She smiled, a faraway look in her eyes. "And mostly because he knew I wanted to live in town."

She paused and took a sip of coffee. "Then we had a few bad weather years. We lost a lot of our herd in a drought. Then, 'bout the time we were pulling out of that, we had a real hard winter. Lost most of the herd in a blizzard that year. For the first time since we'd started, Charles needed help from outside. He went to your uncle."

John nodded. "A lot of help he was."

She reached over and patted his hand, and he had to blink to keep threatening tears at bay. How could she be so kind to him when his uncle had caused her so much pain?

"We didn't like putting up all our holdings as collateral, but we didn't feel we had any choice. Looking back, I've discovered a number of other decisions we could have made, but we didn't—and dwelling on them won't bring him back." She sighed. "Anyway, we put it all up with high hopes that we would pay Harper back early."

"And then another blizzard came." John felt he had to help her get through this. He'd heard enough to know that what the deputy had told him was true.

She nodded. "And we lost more cattle. Harper began pressuring Charles for payment and threatened to foreclose. Finally I believe it just got to be too much. I left Charles up with the books and. . ." She shook her head. She couldn't finish.

Darcie reached for her mother's hand. Tears were running down her face. John had to end it. He was putting them through too much. "I know. You found him the next morning."

Darcie let out a sob, and her mother shook her head. "No. Darcie did."

The breath left John's body as if it had been knocked out of him, and his heart felt as if it would break in two with the pain he felt for these women. He rubbed a hand over his face and pinched the bridge of his nose, trying to get his emotions under control. When he could speak again, all he could say was, "I'm sorry. I'm so sorry. Deputy Johnson told me what Douglas had done to your friends—his wife, Emma, and Liddy McAllister and others in town. Obviously he didn't make it up."

"No, he didn't," Mrs. Malone assured him. "Matt would tell you only the truth."

He took a deep breath and shook his head. "I promise you I will try to make things right if it takes the rest of my life."

Both women wiped their eyes, and Mrs. Malone pulled a handkerchief out of her pocket and blew her nose. "It's not your fault, John. You aren't responsible for the sins of your uncle, and you can't undo the bad he did."

"I have to do what I can to bring honor back to my family's name. I don't even know how to begin to tell my parents about this—the pain Douglas brought to this town. There are so many others—I've got to try to undo some of the harm. And with the Lord's help, I will."

⧫

There was no denying the remorse John must have felt at what his uncle had done. It was all over his face. The sorrow behind the mist of unshed tears in his eyes, the tension around his mouth. His determination to make things right.

He emptied his cup and stood. "I have a lot of work to do. So many records to go over. And I need to let my family know."

Mrs. Malone stood and patted him on the back. "I know that won't be easy for you."

"No. But it's nothing compared to what you've endured because of my father's brother. I—I think I'll go start that letter now."

He headed out the door, then stopped and looked back at them. "Thank you for letting me spend even one night in your home after finding out who I am."

He didn't wait for a reply but turned and hurried into the hallway.

Wiping her eyes again, Darcie's mother reached over and gave her a hug. "That wasn't easy on any of us. But I'm glad he knows the truth, and you finally see—"

"That you and Mrs. Alma were right." Darcie sniffed. "And you were. I was too judgmental, wasn't I?"

"You were. But you know the truth now and, I hope, have learned a valuable lesson about judging others. We can't hold a person responsible for someone else's actions."

Darcie could only nod. She had a lot of soul searching to do. She had been wrong.

Her mother gave her another hug. "I think I'd best go see

if Alma needs a break and help Olivia get ready for bed."

Darcie began to clear the table. "You go on, Mama. I'll finish cleaning up in here."

She needed some time with the Lord. As soon as she was alone, she bowed her head and silently prayed, *Dear Lord, please forgive me for being so wrong. For judging John without even knowing him. I know I need to seek forgiveness from him, too. Please help me find the right way to go about it. And please help him forgive me, too, even though I don't deserve it. Please help me put the hurt in the past and forgive and forget. In Jesus' name, amen.*

It had been so hard to relive all the memories of those turbulent years when her parents were having such a rough time financially. Then finding her papa, collapsed in his office—

Darcie shook her head and plunged her hands into the hot water she'd prepared for washing the last of the dishes. She'd relived it once tonight, and that was enough.

As she washed the cups, she felt the urge to laugh and cry at the same time. Her emotions were nothing if not consistently at war with one another. She felt a bone-deep sorrow that she had judged John so wrongly. At the same time, her heart was soaring with relief that he truly was nothing like his uncle.

And while her mother and Mrs. Alma had been right about him, so it seemed had her heart. It had told her he could be trusted, that he was someone she could fall in love with. Darcie inhaled deeply as she realized she was already there—in love with John—and had been for some time.

She'd been fighting it for weeks now—by trying to convince herself and others he was not to be trusted. By being determined to think ill of him even as she saw with her own eyes that he was a truly good man and nothing like his uncle.

She could fight it no more—she was in love with John Harper. But as suddenly as that admission came to her, so did another thought. And the heart that had been soaring sank to her stomach like a rock. How could John ever love a woman who had made his time in Roswell so difficult by spreading ill will toward him?

thirteen

Darcie came downstairs after spending an almost sleepless night thinking about John and how much he wanted to make amends for his uncle's actions. And how hard she'd made it with her talk over the telephone lines. She'd misused her position at the telephone office and was seriously thinking of resigning as head operator. She didn't deserve the promotion.

But uppermost on her mind was whether or not she could ever right the wrong she'd done to John. Much as she wanted to see him, once she reached the landing, she was almost relieved to hear Olivia's bell tinkling in the back parlor. Her mother hurried out of the kitchen to answer the call, and Darcie waved her back in. "I'll see to Miss Olivia, Mama."

"Thank you, dear. I'm a little late getting things dished up this morning."

"I'll help you," Mrs. Alma said from the stairs. "I'm on my way now."

The bell jingled once more, and Mrs. Alma chuckled. "Your mama is going to rue the day she gave that woman a bell," she whispered to Darcie.

"I think you are right," Darcie whispered back. The bell jingled again. "I'm coming, Miss Olivia."

She hurried into the parlor and was relieved to see that Miss Olivia didn't appear quite as impatient as the bell had sounded. She hadn't slept very well on the settee, though.

Her mother had helped her freshen up earlier, but she felt a little unkempt and wondered if Darcie would help her with her hair.

"Of course I will." She brushed Miss Olivia's hair, taking care to be easy with the tangles. "Will it be more comfortable for you down or in a braid? Or would you like me to put it up into a psyche knot?"

"Let's just go with a braid. I'm afraid the psyche knot would come down with my lounging around, and the braid will keep it neater."

Darcie had to smile. She'd be wanting to look her best, too. "I think that will work very well. If not, you can take it down later in the day."

It didn't take long to braid Miss Olivia's thick hair, and she seemed to feel better once it was done. "Thank you, Darcie. I think I might try to hobble to the dining room now."

"I'll be glad to help you, or if it's too much, I can get one of the men to carry you."

"Would you be a dear and do that? My ankle is still sore and a little stiff."

"I'll be right back." Darcie was disappointed to see that John had already left the table, but Mr. Carlton was still there. He only needed to be asked once. Although he didn't pick her up with the same ease John had, he managed and had her at the table in a few minutes.

"Thank you, sir," Miss Olivia said. "By this evening I hope I can get around myself with the help of those crutches Doc gave me."

Darcie's mother came into the dining room then. "I'll fix Olivia's plate, Darcie, dear. You'd better be getting to your breakfast, or you'll be late for work."

"I'll grab a biscuit and a cup of coffee in the kitchen; then I'll be on my way." Darcie had a feeling her mother would have an extra-busy day dealing with Miss Olivia and her bell. And she thought today Mrs. Alma would either agree to stay because she felt her mother needed her or run as fast as she could back to her own house.

Darcie hoped it was not the latter.

⁂

After mailing the letter he'd written to his family, John left the post office with new determination. A huge weight had lifted from his shoulders since finally talking with the Malones last night. But writing his parents after that about his uncle Douglas and how he'd mistreated the people in this town was one of the hardest things he'd ever done.

One of them. Having to see Darcie and her mother relive even a portion of the pain they'd gone through because of his uncle had been the hardest. No wonder Darcie had been so upset and wanted her mother to throw him out that first night and wished nothing to do with him. He'd have felt the same way. Now he could only pray she would realize he was different from his uncle and maybe someday would return the feelings he had for her. Maybe.

He wished he'd never heard of Douglas Harper or inherited this mess he'd left. But John was determined to make things right in this town. It didn't matter how long it would take or even if he had to use his own money to do it, though he was certain that wouldn't be necessary. His uncle had accumulated a mass of money through the years, and John was going to do his best to give most of it back.

At least now Miss Mead and Elmer were helping him sort through it all. And sort they did. It was a slow process, but Miss Mead filled in the blanks as best she could while Elmer made lists of the people he thought might still live in the vicinity.

John had decided to forgive the outstanding loans and wanted to notify those people so they could live without fear of being harassed for payment or losing their homes to foreclosure. Then there were those who had paid off their loans but had been charged too much interest for late payments. He wanted to pay them back that excess money.

And he truly wanted to find as many people as he could who'd had their land taken away after only one or two late payments and return it to them. He was aware it would take time to make a complete list, to decide what to do with each account, and to find those people still living in the area. He might have to enlist the aid of the sheriff's office or the town council to help, but he would do whatever he had to do to settle the affairs. He was more determined than ever to right the wrongs he could and restore honor to his family's name.

Elmer picked up their lunch from the Roswell Hotel, and they worked until quitting time. From Miss Mead's recollections and her personal notes, he was learning the stories to connect with the names.

There were the Hollingsworths. At first it seemed ridiculous to think his uncle Douglas would want their small ranch. Then Elmer and Miss Mead pointed out it was not far out of town when they'd bought it. Even though they hadn't realized the railroad would eventually run alongside their property, Douglas Harper had known. He figured the town would grow, as it had, and that one day their land would become prime property. If he hadn't gone to jail, he'd have foreclosed on them long ago.

Then there was Benson. He'd had some hard times. An electrical fire had set his place in flames, and he'd had no way to pay back his loan from Harper Bank. When he came to Douglas to ask him to lend him enough to start over and extend the life of the original loan, the man had flatly turned him down. It must have been a blessing to him when Douglas was put in prison.

"Another bank in town loaned him the money to start up again, but I don't know the particulars. He's kept his head above water, but I surely don't think he could pay back both banks," Miss Mead pointed out. "His wife has been sick, too."

"You know them well, Miss Mead?"

"They go to my church, and they've always been real nice to me, even knowing I worked for—"

"My uncle," John finished for her. "I hope you don't mind my asking, but what kept you working for him when you hated the way he did business?"

Miss Mead took off her glasses and rubbed her eyes. "I didn't realize what kind of man he was when I came to work here. He could be very charming, and I fell for that charm. I thought I'd fallen in love with him," she said softly. "He didn't return my feelings. As the years passed, I often wondered if a woman had hurt him at some point in his life. He held most with disregard, nor did it seem to bother him when he made their lives miserable. Of course he didn't single out women. He treated everyone about the same. Awful."

"Yet you kept working for him?"

She shrugged. "I gave him my notice once, but—"

"But what, Miss Mead? Did my uncle threaten you?"

Her slight nod filled him anew with revulsion for his uncle.

"My mother was very ill back East. Her care was costly, and I was paid well. But Douglas threatened to give me a bad recommendation—said I'd never work anywhere else in this town. The family counted on what I sent each month, so I kept working."

"I'm sorry."

"No. It was my fault. I should have left here and gone back East to help take care of her. I could have found a position there. But I still cared for him. I had some notion he would change one day. Hoped I might change him." She put her glasses back on and shook her head. "I made the wrong choice."

"Well, for what it's worth, I'm glad you are here now. I'd never be able to make things right if we hadn't found you."

"I'll take comfort in that, John. Thank you."

John hoped she would. Obviously she'd suffered pain because of his uncle, too.

Miss Mead pulled another stack of papers toward her, then glanced over at him. "I'm starting to believe the Lord kept me here so I could help you with this."

"You may be right. I've been so blessed you agreed to help."

John couldn't help but wonder if Douglas Harper had used the unrequited feelings he held for John's mother as an excuse for the kind of man he became. What a waste. He could have chosen to live a good life with a fine woman who loved him and would have done her best to make him happy. Instead he chose to become a bitter, hateful person determined to bring pain to almost everyone he encountered.

ک

Darcie thought four o'clock would never arrive. It had been one of the longest days she could remember, and she couldn't wait to get out of the office and go home. She'd been fielding more questions about John all day. Hard as she tried to assure everyone he did not have anything to do with the fire and wasn't like his uncle, no one seemed to believe her.

Harriet Howard, one of Roswell's oldest residents, didn't. "What's gotten into you, Darcie? A couple of weeks ago, you wanted to have him thrown out of your mama's boardinghouse. What's changed your mind? I've seen him. He's a right handsome fella. Have you gone and lost your heart to Douglas Harper's kin?"

Darcie was taken aback by her question. And even more by her first thought. *Oh, yes. I'm afraid I have.* Suddenly the irony of it hit her, and she had the urge to laugh. As a chuckle escaped her, she hoped Mrs. Howard took it as an answer.

"Well, I guess you think that's funny, do you?"

"I'm sorry, Mrs. Harriet. I"—*am at a loss for words.* Darcie was thankful when the light lit up over Emma's slot and she could honestly say, "I have to go now. The switchboard is lighting up."

She disconnected the Howard line and inserted a pin into Emma's slot. "Number, please?"

"Darcie, I'm glad I got you."

"What can I do for you, Em?"

"Well, I wanted to check on you. Matt said John Harper paid him a visit yesterday. He seems to think he might not be as bad as we first thought."

"He's right."

"Oh?"

"Mama and I had a long talk with him last night, Em. And she was right. He's not like his uncle. He wants to undo some of the harm Harper did. I was wrong about him and even more wrong to talk about him the way I have."

"Well, who could blame you, Darcie? I certainly understand."

"That doesn't make me right, Em."

"I know. But I was just as bad. I've been suspicious of him ever since I found out who he was. It wasn't just you thinking bad of him."

Darcie knew Emma was trying to make her feel better, but somehow she only felt worse. She changed the subject. "How are you feeling?"

She could hear Emma's sigh over the telephone line before she answered. "I'm excited, tired, and more than ready to have this baby. Doc says any day now."

"Oh! Well, Mama and I are working on Mrs. Alma. We're hoping she's almost ready to make a decision about staying with us."

Emma chuckled. "I sure wish she'd hurry up. But we'll be cozy up here in this apartment until we find something else. I walked past her house today, and it would be so perfect."

"I know. I'll let you know as soon as she makes a decision."

"Thank you. And, Darcie, I truly am glad John isn't like his uncle."

"So am I. I just wish I'd figured it out much earlier. You take care of yourself." She could hear Mandy in the background trying to get Emma's attention. "And give Mandy a hug. She's going to have a big adjustment, isn't she?"

"Yes, but I think she's excited she's going to be a big sister. We'll take special care to give her extra attention, too. Oops! I'd better go! She's trying to reach the cookies—'bye." The line went dead, and Darcie chuckled. Mandy was quite independent at three.

The clock struck four o'clock, and Darcie breathed a sigh of relief. Finally she could go home. She barely said goodbye to her coworkers before she was out the door and headed up the street.

Darcie scarcely felt the balmy May breeze against her skin. Nor did she notice the cloudless blue sky as she walked home. Uppermost on her mind was how to tell John she had played a major role in turning the people of this town against him. She didn't know what she would say, but she wouldn't rest until she told him the truth.

She peeked in on Miss Olivia before going upstairs to change clothes and found her napping, bell clasped tightly in her hand. After changing into a tan skirt and tan-and-white striped blouse a little more appropriate for helping prepare a meal, she took the back stairs that led to the kitchen.

The back door was open to let out some of the heat, and Mrs. Alma was shelling peas at the table while her mother was basting two plump chickens. She returned the roasting pan to the oven and took a seat at the table to help with the peas.

Darcie dropped a kiss on top of her mother's head. "What can I do to help? You two look exhausted."

Mrs. Alma chuckled. "You can see to that bell for the next few hours. I told you your mother would regret giving it to her."

"Oh, Miss Olivia has had you on the run today?" She smiled at her mother's sigh and nod.

"Oh, you could say that," her mother said. "If she's rung that bell one time, she's rung it thirty. She's thirsty—could she have some cool water? She's chilled—could she have a cover? And, oh, would it be too much trouble to make a cup of hot chocolate?"

"And at lunchtime she still felt too wobbly to get to the table—could she have her meal in the parlor?" Mrs. Alma added. "Once we had her settled and came back to our own lunch, that bell jangled again. She was quite lonesome eating by herself—could we join her?"

"I declare, if it wasn't one thing, it was another—all day long. But Olivia is just so sweet about it, you can't really get angry with her." Her mother glanced at the clock. "It's been quiet now for near an hour. I wonder what she's up to?"

"Well, she was napping when I came in. Maybe she'll—"

"No!" Her mother held up her hand and shook her head. "Don't say it. Don't even think it."

Mrs. Alma laughed outright. "She's right. About the time you think it and certainly by the time you get it out of your mouth—"

The bell rang. The two women burst out laughing, and Darcie hurried to see to Miss Olivia, thankful that at least they hadn't lost their sense of humor.

❧

Darcie had wanted to ask John if she could talk to him after dinner, but the only exchange she'd had with him was when he helped bring Miss Olivia to the table. And the conversation at the table pretty much centered on the older woman and how she'd spent her day.

"Mostly I've been keeping Molly and Mrs. Alma on the run. I am so sorry to be so much trouble," Miss Olivia said sweetly.

"We threatened to take her bell away several times, but all in all it wasn't too bad," Mrs. Alma said. "I sat with her for a while and helped her with her knitting. I did decide one thing today."

"Oh?" Darcie's mother said. "What was that?"

"It feels good to be needed. And I was needed today. Olivia is right. It is very lonesome eating alone. I like having company around, too. I like the hustle and bustle here. Well"—she grinned at Olivia—"maybe not that bell, but I do like the other goings-on."

"So what was your decision?" Mr. Carlton prompted.

Mrs. Alma shook her head. "I've decided I don't want to live by myself any longer, so—if the offer to let me stay here is still good, I'll take you up on it."

Darcie's mother jumped to her feet and came around the table to hug her. "Alma, I am so glad! You are needed here. And I love having you around. I am so glad. So glad."

Then Darcie hugged Mrs. Alma. "I am thrilled. It will be so good to have you around all the time."

Mrs. Alma hugged her back. "Well, I must admit, your talk helped convince me. I'd love to be like a grandmother to you."

"Well, you already are. I truly feel that way," Darcie assured her.

"And I'm glad I didn't run you off with my bell," Miss Olivia added.

Mrs. Alma looked happier and healthier than she had in months. Darcie was sure she'd made the right decision.

"What do you want to do about your house?" her mother asked as she passed the bowl of peas. "You know Emma and Matt need a bigger place. Would you be willing to rent it to them for a while? I'm sure they would buy it, if you want to sell, but renting would give you time to be sure."

"Do you think they are still interested?" Mrs. Alma asked Darcie.

"Oh, I know they are—and the sooner the better. Doc says the baby could come anytime now."

"Well, then, I need to talk to them soon as I can."

"Oh, Emma is going to be so excited! She loves your place."

"So do I. But I like it here, too. And my home is too large for me. It was meant for a growing family." Mrs. Alma smiled and nodded. "I think I'd like knowing it was going to someone who loved it as much as I have."

"Would you like me to get Emma on the phone for you?"

"After supper or tomorrow morning will be good enough. She's probably busy right now."

"Well, no matter when you talk to her, you'll make her very happy."

"Just as you've made us," her mother said. "I think this arrangement will work out fine for the lot of us!"

&

Between answering Miss Olivia's bell after dinner, then helping settle her for the night in the back parlor, Darcie had a good idea what her mother and Mrs. Alma had been through that day. She scarcely had time to breathe. And now she wondered when she could talk to John.

When she got back to the kitchen, her mother and Mrs. Alma were finishing up. "I'm sorry. You should have left the cleanup for me."

"You helped plenty by seeing to Olivia for us." Her mother put up the last dish.

"That's for sure." Mrs. Alma chuckled. "I'm plumb tuckered out. I think I'll call it a day."

"Thank you for helping so much, Alma," her mother said. "I don't know what I would have done without you."

Mrs. Alma patted her on the shoulder on her way out of the kitchen. "I should be thanking you. I felt more needed today than I have in years, and I liked the feeling. See you both tomorrow." She turned back to Darcie. "You can telephone Emma and tell her the house is hers if you want to. Tell her we can go over the details tomorrow."

"Oh, Mrs. Alma, she will be so happy. Don't you want to talk to her yourself?"

"Tomorrow is soon enough." She yawned and gave a little wave on her way out the door. "Good night."

Darcie hurried to the telephone to give Emma and Matt the news. Her mother chuckled when she heard Emma's squeal of delight clear across the room. They talked for only a few minutes. Emma told Darcie to let Mrs. Alma know they'd be ready to talk details whenever she was.

"Thank you, my friend," Emma said. "I know you and your mother had a lot to do with this. Please thank her, too."

"I will. We're happy it turned out this way, too."

Darcie hung up the earpiece and grinned. "Needless to say, Emma and Matt are thrilled. They will be so happy in Mrs. Alma's house. And I'm so glad she decided to live here. I think it will be good for her."

"Well, it's certainly going to be good for me," her mother said, hanging up her dish towel.

"Mama, do you know if Mr. Harper has come in from his walk?"

"I don't think so. Why?"

"Last night he apologized to us for his uncle's actions. It's my turn to apologize to him."

Her mother put her arm around her shoulders. "For misjudging him?"

"Yes." And for causing more problems for him by talking about him to anyone who would listen. But she didn't tell her mother that.

"I see."

"I'd sure like to talk to him tonight."

Her mother untied her apron and hung it on a hook by the kitchen door. "You know, I tried all day to find time to sit in the swing on the front porch for a while and relax and smell the scent of the lilacs. How about we go sit a spell in that swing? John is bound to be back soon. When he gets here, I'll leave you to your talk."

fourteen

John was surprised to see both Molly and Darcie swaying back and forth on the front porch swing when he came up the walk. They'd been busy at dinner with Miss Olivia and their other duties, but they both had seemed more comfortable around him since their talk the previous night. Or maybe he was the one who felt more relaxed since he'd discovered the truth about his uncle and apologized.

"Good evening, ladies. It's a beautiful evening to be outside, isn't it?"

"It is. It was a mite stuffy in that kitchen," Mrs. Malone said. "We decided to come outside and relax a bit and enjoy the cool night air."

"It will only be getting warmer in the kitchen in the coming weeks," Darcie said.

Her mother nodded. "We'll be cranking that ice cream churn often."

John leaned against the porch railing and smiled at her. "Did you get Miss Olivia settled down for the night?"

"Well, for a while. I left her reading Harper's Bazaar. She enjoys that magazine so. I'm sure she'll be much more comfortable once she can sleep in her own bed again, but she isn't complaining too much."

"I'm sure she gets bored not being able to get around on her own," John said.

"Alma and I are going to work with her tomorrow and see if we can help her up the stairs. It'll be a start if we can just get her to hobble into another room." Mrs. Malone put her foot down and brought the swing to a stop.

"Be careful, Mama. We don't need you or Mrs. Alma getting hurt."

"I will. Much as I'd like to stay out here with you young people, I guess I'd better go see if Olivia needs anything before she goes to sleep."

"I can go, Mama."

"No, you helped earlier. And you worked all day, too. You deserve to sit awhile. Besides, Alma and I teased her a lot about the bell today. I need to make sure we didn't hurt her feelings."

Darcie watched as her mother went inside. For a moment John half-expected Darcie to follow her mother in, but she didn't. She seemed tired tonight, and he hoped their talk of the night before and all the memories that had been dredged up hadn't given her bad dreams.

"Did you have a hard day, Miss Darcie?"

"It—was a long day." Darcie put the swing in motion again but only for a moment before she brought it to a stop. She looked over at him. "Mr. Harper. . .I—"

"Please—call me John. Right this moment I am not too fond of my last name."

"I'm sorry. I—"

She had no reason to be sorry for that. "It's certainly not your fault, Miss Darcie."

"No, not your last name, but—" She paused and took a deep breath before continuing. "Mr.—uh—John, I—would like to talk to you, if you have the time."

"Of course I have the time." Darcie seemed nervous, and he wanted to put her at ease. "What can I do for you?"

"Nothing. It's not what you can do for me. I need to—"

She paused again and stood, then joined him at the porch rail. "I need to apologize to you."

"To me? Miss Darcie, what could you possibly need to apologize to me for?"

She looked down at the floor of the porch and exhaled before speaking. "I'm afraid I've had a hand in turning some of the people of Roswell against you. I couldn't stand that a relative of Douglas Harper was living under my mother's roof, and I used my position at the telephone company to—"

Disappointment settled deep inside him, but he couldn't be angry with her. "I understand."

And he did. As sorry as he was that she hadn't seen he was unlike his uncle, he could appreciate how she'd assumed he wasn't. And he couldn't blame her, not really. After all he'd found out about Douglas Harper, the horrible things he'd done, and now that he knew it was Darcie who had found her father—John could not blame her for feeling the way she did. He could only wish things were different as his hopes for the future suddenly seemed dim.

"You may understand," Darcie said, looking him in the eye. "But that doesn't make what I did right. I am truly sorry I've made your time here even more unpleasant than it needed to be. I—I don't know what else to say, except that one day I hope you can forgive me."

With those words, Darcie turned and ran back into the house, leaving him to ponder her words. It did pain him that she'd thought so little of him and told everyone so, but he admired her honesty now.

John turned and gazed up at the star-studded sky. He breathed deeply, and the scent of lilacs hit his nostrils—sweet and delicate, like Darcie. Except she wasn't that delicate. She'd been through a lot in her life and was stronger than she thought. She'd been determined to tell him the truth tonight and apologize. Could she feel differently about him now? Could she finally be realizing he truly wanted to undo some of the harm his uncle had done?

A flicker of hope stirred in his heart. Maybe he could have a future in this town after all.

❧

Darcie was glad she didn't run into anyone as she hurried back inside and up the stairs. Her heart had twisted in pain at the hurt she saw in John's eyes when she told him what she had done.

Fresh tears welled up as she entered her room and knelt at her window seat. How awful she must seem to him. He'd come here to settle his uncle's estate and had no idea of the corruption he would uncover. He was already hurting after finding out what his uncle had done. He wanted desperately to make amends to this town, and now it must seem she had gone out of her way to make trouble for him.

Darcie wept. In her own way, she was no better than John's uncle. She'd sinned, too—by judging John because he was related to Douglas Harper and then spreading ill will toward him. Whatever dreams she'd woven from that first night she met him, to the ones she'd only recently let herself dream again, had disappeared into the air because of her actions. She hadn't trusted him because of his uncle's deeds. But now how could John ever trust her—after her own? And how could she have the audacity to ask him to forgive her when she realized she must forgive his uncle?

Feeling as if her heart would break, Darcie prayed.

"Dear Father, please forgive me. I have been guilty of judging John so wrongly, and I've caused him pain because of it. I've made the work he's trying to do much harder. I've fought my feelings for him because of who he was related to, when I should have accepted him for who he is and recognized what my heart was telling me—what You were trying to get through to me. He is a good and honorable man, and I'll never find another like him. I pray that one day he will forgive me, too, even though I don't deserve it. I know I've destroyed any hope for a future with him. Father, please, please help me to find a way to make things right for him— to convince people I was wrong about him. Please help me, Father, to forgive Douglas Harper and put the past behind me. Your will be done. In Jesus' name, amen."

Darcie stood, wiped her eyes, and blew her nose. It was time to quit feeling sorry for herself. She may not have a future with John, but that didn't cancel the love she felt for him. She must find a way to undo some of her own wrongs. She had to find a way to convince the town John was trying to help them, not harm them.

She would sleep on it, knowing she would have an answer soon as to what to do. The Lord would help her, of that she had no doubt.

ప

John hoped Darcie slept better than he did, but when he finally saw her, the dark circles under her eyes told him she probably hadn't. He wished he could assure her he harbored no ill will toward her and might have done the same under similar circumstances.

But he had no chance to talk to her this morning, what with her helping her mother with Miss Olivia first thing, then rushing off to work. He left for the bank, assuring himself he would make it a point to tell her he forgave her— before the day was out if he could.

Knowing what he was up against, after Darcie's confession

to him, somehow made it easier to accept the people's reactions on seeing him. One person darted across the road while another ducked into the nearest business to avoid passing by him. Then others kept walking but didn't look at him or speak.

Instead of accommodating them by staying silent today, he tipped his hat, smiled, and said, "Good morning."

Several people looked a little surprised at his overture, but it didn't bother John. He finally understood why they'd treated him the way they had. Oh, Darcie thought it had a lot to do with her, and maybe she hadn't helped his cause, but they treated him the way they did because of his uncle's treatment of them and this town.

One of these days—soon, he hoped—they would see he meant them no harm. In the meantime he'd keep going through records and ledgers until he had as clear a picture as possible before he started contacting people. And he would keep praying he had the answers he needed soon, so he could make things right.

Elmer and Miss Mead could probably tell he was getting impatient because they worked as diligently as possible. They worked well together, and the new stack of records they were compiling began to overtake the old ones. The end might be in sight after all.

He prayed again that once he began making reparations, he could convince Darcie to give him a chance to win her heart. But that would have to wait until he could show the town a man couldn't and shouldn't be judged by his relatives.

❧

Darcie called Emma, Liddy, and Beth and asked if they could meet for tea that afternoon. She was determined not to use her position at the telephone office to talk about this or anything else over the lines. If she messed up again—well, she would have to resign.

But when several people asked her about John, she took that opportunity to tell them she'd been wrong. That John Harper wasn't anything like his uncle and she should never have talked about him the way she did. And that she wasn't going to discuss him anymore. And she meant it.

But others in town had taken her words to their friends and neighbors, probably elaborating with each telling, as Darcie knew could happen. She wasn't sure how she'd ever reach them all when she didn't know who had been told.

But an idea was forming in her mind, and she wanted her friends' opinion about it. She watched the clock all afternoon, anxious to get to Emma's Café. While word would spread that she was now defending John, she didn't want him to have to wait. No. She needed to do more. And as quickly as possible.

When she arrived at the café, her friends were waiting for her upstairs in Emma's apartment. The children were playing happily together, and Darcie was pleased to have more privacy than the café would have offered.

Darcie had already told them she thought she'd been wrong about John and needed their help in finding a way to convince the town of the same.

"You're certain he isn't here to hurt the town, Darcie?" Liddy asked. "And what about the fire?"

"I'm certain. John had nothing to do with that fire. He only wants to make things right from his uncle. Mama and I talked to him the other night, and I'm certain he's being honest with us."

"I have to agree with Darcie," Emma said. "Matt told me they've determined the fire was an accident and that John had nothing to do with it. Matt thinks he is sincere in wanting to help the people of Roswell, and he's agreed to help John locate as many people as he can."

"Well, I am relieved and happy he is nothing like his uncle," Beth said. "Jeb said the way he helped with that fire told him a lot about the man, and he couldn't believe he was here to bring pain to anyone."

Just me. Darcie quickly chided herself for the thought. John hadn't been the one to bring her pain. She'd brought it on herself. If she'd followed her heart's lead that first night, she wouldn't be going through this heartache now. Instead she had to accept the fact there was probably no way they could ever have a future together.

Liddy sighed deeply. "Well, I'm just plain relieved. I found it a little hard to believe he was like his uncle. Douglas was the worst kind of man. I couldn't see that in John."

"If I hadn't spread the word about him, probably no one else would, either," Darcie said, shaking her head.

"Oh, I don't know about that, Darcie," Emma said. "Emotions run very high against Douglas Harper in this town. I think he'd probably have gotten the same reaction no matter how they found out who John was."

Darcie looked at Beth. "I'm sorry, Beth. I know you tried to drill into me not to spread gossip along the lines, and I truly intended to be like you when I got my promotion. I'm sorry I've disappointed you, too."

"Oh, Darcie, I do understand. I know all too well how easy it is for customers to draw one into talking about the things they want to know. Don't you remember when Jeb and I were at odds about the children and then falling in love? The whole town seemed to have an opinion on what we should do."

"But that doesn't excuse my actions. They were giving you

their opinion, not the other way around."

"No, it doesn't. It was wrong, but you went through so much because of Douglas Harper—and then to have his nephew living under the same roof." Beth shook her head. "I'm not sure I could have done any better. And through all of this, I think you've learned a valuable lesson."

Oh, yes, she had. One she didn't think she would ever forget. Darcie was relieved her friends had come to the right conclusion about John, without her having to convince them, and she told them of her plan to get the town to accept him.

"I think that is a wonderful idea, Darcie," Beth said, smiling.

"I hope it will work. I have to do something."

"Well, it would certainly be a way to get the word out quickly and to as many as possible at one time," Emma said.

Darcie breathed a sigh of relief that they were willing to help her, and she silently thanked the Lord for the friends He'd given her. They were always so supportive.

"I don't know what I'd do without you all!"

"I'll telephone Matt now. Maybe he and the sheriff can help with this." Emma stood and hurried—as much as she could in her condition—into the kitchen to make her call.

Liddy's youngest let out a yelp just then, and she rushed to see to him, leaving Darcie and Beth at the table. Darcie had noticed Beth watching her closely as they all talked. Now she took advantage of the time they had alone to ask, "You're beginning to care about John, aren't you, Darcie?"

Beginning to? Hardly. But she wasn't ready to admit her feelings to her friend yet. "After the way I've tried to turn everyone against him, Beth, it wouldn't do me any good to care now, would it?"

"Oh, Darcie." Beth chuckled. "If Jeb could forgive me for misjudging him and causing him to fall off the roof and break his arm, I'm sure John can forgive you for any trouble you've caused him."

Beth's words caused hope to flare in Darcie's heart. But then she recalled the hurt she'd seen in his eyes and tamped it back down. She couldn't let herself think about that now. All she could concentrate on was getting out the truth. With the sheriff's and Matt's help, she hoped she could do that soon.

❧

The next few days were filled with frustration for John. Matters were going well at the bank, and he had almost all the information he needed to begin contacting people; but at the boardinghouse, Darcie seemed to be avoiding him. She stayed busy helping her mother in the kitchen and around the house and helping with Miss Olivia or working. On Thursday her chair was empty as they sat down for dinner.

"Where is Darcie?" Miss Olivia asked. "She's awfully late today."

"She'll be here soon," her mother said. "The city council has called a meeting for tomorrow night, and the telephone company has been asked to get out the word. It's open to the public. We'll be having an early dinner because I want to attend."

"What's the purpose of the meeting?" Mr. Carlton asked.

"I'm not sure, but it's been awhile since we've had an open council meeting. I think we all should try to go."

"Oh." Miss Olivia looked dismayed. "I'm not sure I—"

"Don't worry, Olivia," Mrs. Alma said. "We'll get you there."

John had never heard of a city council meeting being called like this. At home the newspapers carried a notice about a week in advance; this seemed like short notice to him. But then Roswell wasn't that large, and he supposed they had a different way of doing things out West.

Darcie breezed in then. "I'm so sorry I'm late. I'll wash up and join you." After a few minutes, she returned and hurried to take her seat at the table.

She looked tired to John but more at ease than he'd seen her. He couldn't help but wonder what had caused it. She even smiled at him when she thanked him for handing her the platter of fried chicken. He loved that smile and hoped he'd have a chance to tell her how much one day soon.

"Miss Darcie, can you tell us what the meeting is about?" Mr. Mitchell asked, drawing Darcie's attention to him.

She glanced at her mother before answering, and John wondered if she knew more about it than she'd be willing to tell.

"I think the council wants to address several things. We probably just need to be there to find out, Mr. Mitchell. I know I plan on going."

"Are you going, Mr. Harper?" Miss Olivia asked.

"Oh, I'm not sure. I'm not actually a citizen of Roswell—"

"It's open to everyone," Mrs. Alma put in. "You ought to come. Our city council meetings have always been interesting. I'm anxious to find out why they'd call a special meeting open to us all."

Darcie hurried through the meal, then excused herself. He had a strong feeling she was trying to avoid running into him, because he didn't glimpse that smile for the rest of the evening.

⋧

John didn't see Darcie the next morning, either, and he left for work with a heavy heart. Even though Darcie realized he was not the ogre she'd first thought him to be and despite the fact she'd apologized for expressing her opinion of him to many in town, she still evidently had no wish to know him better.

Elmer and Miss Mead were waiting at the bank for him,

and they started to work right away. At the pace they were going since Charlotte Mead began helping them, John figured he'd have a complete set of records to work from by early the next week. And, odd as it sounded even to his ears, he couldn't wait to start giving away his inheritance. He hoped nothing was left of his uncle's money, and if anything was left after he settled accounts, he would find a good cause to support. He wanted none of it for himself.

Midmorning, Deputy Matt Johnson entered the bank, and John was pleased to see him. He'd offered to help locate as many people as he could, and John had a list almost ready to give to him.

"Mr. Harper, how's it going?"

"Please call me John. It's going well. We're making a list of people I might need help in finding. I should be able to have it to you by early next week."

The deputy nodded. "That's good. I'm sure you'll be glad to get all this behind you."

"More than I can say." He could never put his uncle's past behind him and get on with his life until it was settled.

"I thought I'd just check in and see if you needed anything, but I can see you have everything under control."

John chuckled. It sure didn't seem that way to him. "Looks can be deceiving, you know."

The deputy laughed on his way out the door. He waved good-bye to Elmer and Miss Mead. "See you all tonight."

John wasn't sure he'd be going. He didn't know what the meeting was about, and though he was curious, he didn't think he'd be welcome there. But when he got back to the boardinghouse that afternoon and checked his mail, he was surprised to find an invitation from the city council to attend tonight's meeting.

"Did you get a special invitation, Mrs. Malone?" he asked her when she called everyone to an early dinner.

"No, I didn't. Maybe you received one because you're working in your uncle's bank and they think you might be starting it up again."

"Hmm." *More likely they want to run me out of town.* A few weeks ago, he would have been relieved to go home. But now he had come to like Roswell and was seriously thinking of staying and setting up business. In spite of what his head told him, his heart was still hoping for a future with Darcie Malone.

"Will you attend?" Mrs. Malone asked.

"Well, how can I turn down a special invitation?"

She smiled at him. "I'd certainly find it hard to. I've rented a surrey to take Olivia there, and we'll have room for all of us. Darcie went to help Emma pack up some things so they can move over to Alma's this weekend. She'll stay in town and have supper with Emma and Matt and go to the meeting with them."

John's mind was made up. The only way he would probably see Darcie tonight was to go to that meeting.

fifteen

Darcie had met with several city council members over the last few days. Until then she hadn't realized how many residents of Roswell had been letting the councilmen know their feelings about Douglas Harper's nephew being there. After her meeting with them, they'd all expressed admiration for how she was trying to help settle some of the tension in their town.

When she arrived with Emma and Matt, Mayor Adams motioned for her to come to the front of the room and take a seat with the council. She was aware they expected much good to come from this town meeting. She took a seat and gazed out over the room; she hoped they were right.

Earlier her mother had telephoned Emma's to let her know John would be there. Darcie didn't think she'd ever been more nervous in her life as she waited for her mother and the rest of the boarders to show up. She just wanted to get through this night.

From her vantage point, she could see her mother, John, and the other boarders arriving. They found the seats Emma and Matt and her friends had saved for them and waved to Darcie as they sat down. Even with all the support she had in this room, Darcie turned to the One who would help her best. She sent up a silent prayer that she would be able to say what she needed to so the town would accept John for who he was.

The room had filled up fast. The mayor called the meeting

159

to order, and Darcie took a deep breath as she waited for her introduction.

"We've called this meeting tonight because of an unusual request. After talking to one of our good citizens at length, it seemed the best way to put a bad period for this town to rest was to call an open town meeting. The board and I would like to welcome you all and especially Miss Darcie Malone to our meeting tonight. Without further discussion, I will yield the floor to Miss Malone."

Darcie rubbed her moist palms against her skirt and walked over to the lectern amid applause from the audience. Friends, neighbors, acquaintances, and others she'd never even seen before—she hoped they would all take to heart what she had to say.

Uncomfortable with the attention focused on her, she smiled and nodded her head at the councilmen before she began. "Thank you, Mayor and councilmen. I appreciate your quick response to my request."

She turned back to the room full of people. "I thank you all for coming tonight. I'm here to try to set a few misconceptions to rest—I hope for the good of us all."

She took a deep breath and looked out over the room. Her mother was giving her a heartening nod, while Beth encouraged her with a smile. Emma and Liddy were clapping and smiling. John seemed a bit confused, as did most of the others in the audience. But his gaze never left her as she began to talk.

"There aren't many in this room who do not know who Douglas Harper was, who weren't hurt in some way by him. And many of you know his nephew is here now, trying to—"

"Stir up trouble for us all again!" someone yelled from the back of the room.

"Or get money we don't have!" someone else called out from another direction.

"Or take our land!" another person shouted.

Darcie raised her hand and shook her head. "No, no! You have it all wrong. Please—listen to what I have to say." She sighed with relief when the room quieted.

"John Harper is not here to do anyone harm," she continued. "And I am afraid it is because of me that many of you think he might be. I was wrong to stir up trouble. From the first, I saw only that he was Douglas Harper's relative, and I assumed he was no better than his uncle. I've made no secret of how I felt about that man. But I was wrong to judge his nephew. John Harper is nothing like Douglas. All he wants to do is try to make things right—if we will let him."

Darcie looked out into the room. John was sitting forward in his seat beside her mother, his gaze steady on her. Her heart beating rapidly, she had to finish, had to get the words out. She looked into John's eyes and said the words the people of Roswell needed to hear. "Mr. Harper, I owe you and the whole town an apology for any hard feelings I stirred up. I am truly sorry for the trouble I've caused you. I've recently realized I need to forgive Douglas Harper and put all of that pain in the past, and I hope you will also forgive me."

She looked back toward the audience. "I hope you all will forgive me."

With that, Darcie turned back to the mayor and smiled, her palms spread wide. "I have no more to say."

Mayor Adams took her place as she hurried back to her seat. He cleared his throat. "Miss Malone, I think I speak for the whole council when I thank you for your honesty and for trying to bring good will back to our town.

"This city needs to put certain things in the past, also. I

hope we can do that now." He looked into the audience. "I believe we should let Mr. Harper have a say, if he's a mind to."

⁂

John was stunned by Darcie's public apology. Now his heart slammed against his chest at the realization that this woman cared enough about him to stand up in front of these people and defend him. That she finally did realize he was totally different from his uncle.

His heart soared as he stood and nodded. While he strode to the front, he half-expected some of the men to drag him away. Instead the room was quiet while he approached the mayor.

Mayor Adams shook his hand and motioned for him to address the crowd. Darcie gave him a sweet half smile, encouraging him enough to stand up in front of the room full of people. People who didn't want to have a thing to do with him but were willing to listen to him because of Darcie.

The tension in the room was thick while everyone waited for him to speak. John looked out at the crowd and back to Darcie. Seeing the sorrow in her eyes, he smiled at her. "Miss Darcie, there is nothing to forgive. After everything I've found out about Douglas Harper, I can understand why you would be suspicious of anyone with the same last name. Many times in the last few weeks I have wished my last name was not Harper."

He heard a twitter or two and maybe even a chuckle as he turned back to the room. "My—uncle—treated the people in this town abominably, and there is no way I can apologize to you all enough for his actions. But I want to make amends as best I can. I've been going over the bank records, and I'm to a point now where I think I can start to do that."

Several people in the room began to speak softly to one

another as he continued. "I'd like to ask those of you who were affected by my uncle's business practices to come by the office as soon as it is convenient for you so I can begin to set things right. For those of you who feel you owed my uncle money, I plan on marking those debts paid."

A collective gasp went up over the room while John kept talking. "For those of you who feel Douglas Harper overcharged you or owed you money, I will strive to make things right—no matter how long it takes."

"And"—John spoke louder to be heard over the excited whispers that were spreading across the room in a wave—"if you had land and property taken away"—the murmuring stopped, and total quiet ensued—"I would like to see you get it back if possible. I want to make Roswell my home, but before I can do that, I must make amends to as many as I can and bring honor back to my family name."

With that, the room erupted with thundering applause, and for the first time since he had arrived in the town, John felt welcomed.

૨ે

When the meeting was dismissed, Darcie watched the council members and more than a few from the audience approach John and either clap him on the shoulder, shake his hand, or say something with a smile. She felt an immense relief that things might change for him now.

She turned to greet Emma, Liddy, Beth, and their husbands as they came up and congratulated her on being so courageous and honest.

"Without your support, I don't think I could have done it. Thank you all," Darcie said. The friends the Lord had put into her life had truly blessed her.

They were just making plans to get together the next day

when Emma gasped and held on to Matt.

"Another pain?" Matt asked. At her nod, he looked across the room. "I think it's time we find Doc Bradshaw. Emma's been having pains for the last few hours, but nothing would do her but to be here."

"Oh, Em! You go see about yourself now, you hear?" Darcie said.

"We'll see to her, Darcie," Liddy said as she and Cal took off behind Matt, who was leading Emma as gently and fast as he could over to the doctor.

Beth looked as if she wasn't sure whether to stay with Darcie or hurry after Emma. In her condition, Darcie could understand her wanting to go. She shooed her in that direction. "Go on. Just let me know when she has the baby, all right?"

Beth hugged her. "I will. This is so exciting!" She grabbed Jeb by the hand, and they took off across the room.

Darcie turned in the other direction and headed over to where her mother and the boarders were waiting for her. Her mother enveloped her in a hug. "That was a wonderful thing you did, dear. Your papa would have been so very proud of you, just as I am."

"Me, too, Darcie! I feel like a proud grandma tonight," Mrs. Alma added as she hugged Darcie.

"Thank you, Mama and Mrs. Alma. I wish it hadn't been necessary and that I hadn't—" She felt a touch on her shoulder and turned to find John looking at her. The expression in his eyes sent her heart dropping into her stomach and back up again to hammer against her ribs.

"Miss Darcie, I can't thank you enough for what you've done for me tonight." John touched his chest and smiled at her. "I feel I have a new start here because of what you did."

She shook her head. "I only did what I should have done

from the very start. Had I not—"

"Tonight you made up for any harm you think you might have done," John said, looking deep into her eyes. "I—uh— I'd like to see you home, if I may?"

Darcie smiled and nodded.

John turned to her mother. "Mrs. Malone, would it be all right with you if I saw your daughter home?"

Darcie's mother looked from one to the other before Mrs. Alma nudged her on the shoulder. "Oh, Molly, let the young man see Darcie home. You know he'll get her there safely," the older woman insisted.

"All right." Mrs. Malone smiled and nodded. "Yes, John. You may see Darcie home. But don't dawdle."

"Do you need help with Miss Olivia before we leave?" John asked politely.

"No. Mr. Carlton and Mr. Mitchell can help us get home. We'll see you there." Mrs. Malone started to lead her boarders to the door, then turned back. "I was proud of you both tonight."

Darcie could see how much those words meant to John by the look on his face. He cared about her mother; she prayed he cared about her, too. As he gripped her elbow and led her up the aisle, she had a feeling their relationship had changed in some imperceptible way. She prayed it was in the direction she'd been dreaming of but was afraid to hope too much.

As they walked out into the evening air, Darcie wished she'd thought to bring a shawl with her. It didn't seem to matter how warm it was during the day in New Mexico Territory, the night air turned cool. John looked at her then and smiled, pulling her hand through his arm as they left City Hall, and Darcie didn't notice the temperature quite so much.

Strolling down the street, John seemed surprised when

several people leaving the meeting called out for them to have a good evening, some of the men tipping their hats to them.

"What a difference a day makes," John said. "I'd about given up hope of ever being greeted in a friendly manner in this town."

Darcie's heart felt near breaking at the way she—and the whole town—had treated him. But she was grateful for what had happened tonight. They turned the corner and headed down Fourth Street.

"Anyway, it feels good. And it's all due to you—"

She took a deep breath and shook her head. "No. All that pain was due to me, and I am so sorry for my part in—"

John stopped and turned toward her. Looking deep into her eyes, he said, "Shh. Let's leave that in the past where it belongs."

That's what Darcie wanted to do—with all her heart. But could John?

"I can't begin to tell you how it felt to walk into that room tonight." He chuckled. "For a moment I was pretty sure I was going to be run out of town. But then I saw you and—Darcie, you were so lovely up there and you spoke so eloquently that you took my breath away. You were wonderful, and suddenly I knew everything would be all right."

Darcie's heart almost melted as John gazed deep into her eyes. He'd forgiven her—she knew he had—yet she still needed to say more. "I—if I can do any more to help the people of this town accept you—"

"The only person I want to accept me right now is you." His voice was deep and husky. "But there is one thing more you could do for me, if you are of a mind to."

Darcie felt as if her heart would pound out of her chest as he pulled her into the circle of his arms. "What—what is that?"

He tipped her face up to his. "I love you, Miss Darcie Malone, with all my heart. And if you would consent to marry me, you would make me the happiest man in New Mexico Territory."

John loved her. Darcie felt it deep inside. And if that weren't enough, the love shining in his eyes was so strong and bright that it nearly took her breath away. But not before she uttered, "Yes, oh, yes, I will marry you, John Harper."

John's lips claimed hers with a kiss that promised he would cherish her all the days of their lives—and far surpassed any dreams she had woven when her heart told her the truth of how she felt.

Darcie wrapped her arms around John's neck and kissed him back, thanking the Lord for showing them both how to go about making amends.

epilogue

June 1899

Darcie stopped at the landing and prepared to walk down the rest of the stairs in Malone's Boardinghouse for the last time as Darcie Malone. She still couldn't believe it was her wedding day. What was even more unbelievable to her was that in a few minutes she would be marrying the nephew of the man who had been responsible for giving her family and the whole town of Roswell a great deal of heartache.

Soon she would be Darcie Marie Harper—Mrs. John Harper—wife of the most wonderful man in the world. That she was marrying the nephew of Douglas Harper still had her shaking her head in amazement, and she had to stifle a giggle at the irony. The Lord had a wonderful sense of humor.

Darcie was sure old Douglas would turn over in his grave if he knew she was about to marry his nephew, John Harper. But there was not a doubt in her mind that marrying John was exactly what the Lord had intended when He brought him to Roswell—to marry her and set right in this town what his uncle had done wrong.

But Douglas Harper, who had done so much harm in Roswell, would not be happy or laughing right now. He would hate the fact that his nephew had used all the money he'd left him to pay back to the citizens of Roswell what Douglas had taken away. Nor would he be celebrating the fact that, because of everything John was doing, this town could finally get over the bitterness and hate they'd felt toward anyone with the Harper name.

In the past few weeks, land had been returned to some rightful owners, debts had been forgiven, and excess interest paid back. And Darcie was about to marry the love of her life.

Now, as her mother signaled to her to start the wedding march down the last short flight of stairs, Darcie's heart filled with so much love and thankfulness, she thought it surely would burst with joy.

She spotted her friends and neighbors waiting to witness her and John exchange their vows. She was struck once more at how true it was that all things work together for good to them that love God—and that vengeance was His. She could see God's work in her life and the way He'd brought her and John together. And she had no doubt He had worked in the lives of her friends.

Liddy and Cal had a wonderful home and family they'd blended together. Had it not been for the Lord protecting Liddy from Douglas Harper's plans to take her land, they might never have met and fallen in love.

Had it not been for the Lord putting an end to Douglas's hateful plans to run Emma out of town and get her property, Emma and Matt Johnson might not have fallen in love and made a home for Mandy—and given her a new little sister.

Even Beth and Jeb Winslow had benefited from the Lord's condemnation of Douglas Harper's business practices. If it hadn't been for Him giving the Nordstroms the determination not to let Douglas have their place, selling out to Jeb's brother Harland instead, they wouldn't have the lovely home they'd worked hard to refurbish for their growing family.

No, Douglas Harper would have liked none of that. And

it no longer mattered. Even Darcie had forgiven the man for the hurt he caused her family. For as she met John at the bay window in her mother's front parlor, gazed into his eyes, and exchanged wedding vows with him, she realized her heart had no room for hate. It was far too full of love for another man named Harper.

Darcie's heart soared with joy as Minister Turley pronounced them husband and wife.

John lifted her veil and raised her face to his. "I love you," he whispered.

"I love you, too," Darcie whispered back.

He bent his head, and they kissed, sealing their vows and assuring one another that they had made amends and started their future together.

A Letter To Our Readers

Dear Reader:

In order that we might better contribute to your reading enjoyment, we would appreciate your taking a few minutes to respond to the following questions. We welcome your comments and read each form and letter we receive. When completed, please return to the following:

Fiction Editor
Heartsong Presents
PO Box 719
Uhrichsville, Ohio 44683

1. Did you enjoy reading *Making Amends* by Janet Lee Barton?
   ❑ Very much! I would like to see more books by this author!
   ❑ Moderately. I would have enjoyed it more if

   _____

   _____

   _____

2. Are you a member of **Heartsong Presents**? ❑ Yes ❑ No
   If no, where did you purchase this book? _____

   _____

3. How would you rate, on a scale from 1 (poor) to 5 (superior), the cover design? _____

4. On a scale from 1 (poor) to 10 (superior), please rate the following elements.

   ____ Heroine   ____ Plot
   ____ Hero   ____ Inspirational theme
   ____ Setting   ____ Secondary characters

5. These characters were special because?_____

_____

_____

6. How has this book inspired your life?_____

_____

_____

7. What settings would you like to see covered in future
   Heartsong Presents books? _____

_____

_____

8. What are some inspirational themes you would like to see
   treated in future books? _____

_____

_____

9. Would you be interested in reading other **Heartsong
   Presents** titles? ❏ Yes   ❏ No

10. Please check your age range:
    ❏ Under 18   ❏ 18-24
    ❏ 25-34   ❏ 35-45
    ❏ 46-55   ❏ Over 55

Name_____

Occupation _____

Address _____

Heart♥ng

Presents

HEARTSONG
PRESENTS

If you love Christian romance...

You'll love Heartsong Presents' inspiring and faith-filled romances by today's very best Christian authors...DiAnn Mills, Wanda E. Brunstetter, and Yvonne Lehman, to mention a few!

$10.99

When you join Heartsong Presents, you'll enjoy 4 brand-new mass market, 176-page books—two contemporary and two historical—that will build you up in your faith when you discover God's role in every relationship you read about!

Imagine...four new romances every four weeks—with men and women like you who long to meet the one God has chosen as the love of their lives...all for the low price of $10.99 postpaid.

Mass Market 176 Pages

To join, simply visit www.heartsong presents.com or complete the coupon below and mail it to the address provided.

✂ -

YES! Sign me up for Heart♥ng!

NEW MEMBERSHIPS WILL BE SHIPPED IMMEDIATELY!
Send no money now. We'll bill you only $10.99 post-paid with your first shipment of four books. Or for faster action, call 1-740-922-7280.

NAME _____

ADDRESS _____

CITY _____ STATE _____ ZIP _____

MAIL TO: HEARTSONG PRESENTS, P.O. Box 721, Uhrichsville, Ohio 44683
or sign up at WWW.HEARTSONGPRESENTS.COM